'Antonia…you're beautiful…'

Pulling back, Rafe buried his face in her throat, his hands sliding beneath her shirt to roam restlessly across her back and then to her midriff, half circling her ribcage, smoothing upwards, until his thumbs stroked the soft underswell of her breasts.

They kissed again, and with a passion she'd hardly known she possessed she kissed him back, opening her mouth to his, inviting him in to all her secret places, tasting him all over again.

'We could skip the party…'

Rafe's meaning was clear and Toni felt a fluttering inside, her mind zeroing in on the fact that they were alone and there was no one there to disturb them. Whatever they chose to do…

'I want to be with you, Antonia…' His hands stroked up her arms before he gathered her in again, holding her to him so that she felt the imprint of him from thigh to breast.

'Rafe…' She gusted a small indrawn breath, feeling his hands on her lower back, tilting her closer still, and the sweet sting of anticipation slithered up her spine

'Just say the word.' His voice was muffled against her hair.

Toni took a breath so deep it almost hurt. Could she? Dared she? Winding her arms around his neck, she closed her eyes, picturing him as her lover, dreaming of his body claiming hers so completely, so fully.

So honestly.

And when he took her mouth again the feeling of oneness was so intense, so tangible, she almost gave the answer he wanted to hear. But a little voice in her head kept insisting that once they'd taken that step there was no going back. Nothing would be simple between them again…

Leah Martyn loves to create warm, believable characters for the Medical Romance™ series. She is grounded firmly in rural Australia, and the special qualities of the bush are reflected in her stories. For plots and possibilities, she bounces ideas off her husband on their early-morning walks. Browsing in bookshops and buying an armful of new releases is high on her list of enjoyable things to do.

REDEEMING
DR RICCARDI

BY
LEAH MARTYN

First published in Great Britain 2012
by Mills & Boon, an imprint of Harlequin (UK) Limited.
Harlequin (UK) Limited, Eton House, 18-24 Paradise Road,
Richmond, Surrey TW9 1SR

© Leah Martyn 2012

ISBN: 978 0 263 22892 2

Harlequin (UK) policy is to use papers that are natural, renewable and recyclable products and made from wood grown in sustainable forests. The logging and manufacturing process conform to the legal environmental regulations of the country of origin.

Printed and bound in Great Britain
by CPI Antony Rowe, Chippenham, Wiltshire

Previous titles by Leah Martyn:

DAREDEVIL AND DR KATE
WEDDING IN DARLING DOWNS
OUTBACK DOCTOR, ENGLISH BRIDE

**These books are also available in eBook format
from www.millsandboon.co.uk**

For Zach, Hannah, Ava and Raphael.
'You are so beautiful.'

CHAPTER ONE

VALENTINE'S DAY had fallen on a Monday. And who on earth felt like partying on a Monday?

All the off-duty staff at the hospital apparently.

Nurse Manager Toni Morell's mouth lifted in a wry little twist, as she swung into the car park at the district hospital. For years now, Valentine's had been the day set aside for the annual fundraiser organised by the social committee and excuses for non-attendance were not allowed.

Toni just hoped she'd have enough energy at the end of her shift to get herself into party mode. It was her first day back from leave, and while her time in Sydney had been fun, it was nice to be back in the less hectic pace of the rural town of Forrestdale, where she'd now chosen to make her life.

As she gathered her bag from the passenger seat, her thoughts flew to the day ahead. Accident and Emergency had a new relieving senior registrar, Rafe Riccardi. Toni had spoken with him only briefly at the end of her shift before she'd taken off on holidays.

When they'd met, he'd been surrounded by board members and there had been no opportunity for a longer chat. But she recalled his handshake had been firm and he'd looked her in the eye. And she'd thought later that he could be described as tall, dark and…not handsome exactly but there'd been something about him, a *presence* that would be hard to ignore. Toni just hoped he was proving a good fit for their team. Her tummy swooped slightly. Staff changes at senior level always came with a niggle of uncertainty. But it wasn't as though Dr Riccardi was here for ever. He had a three-month contract while he covered long-service leave for their usual reg, Joe Lyons.

Toni's mind clicked into work mode as she made her way along to the staffroom. She'd left home in plenty of time, determined to get a jump start and catch up on things generally.

But it seemed as though the entire shift had arrived early as well and the place was buzzing. A love song was pumping out from the local radio station, helium-filled red hearts were floating against the ceiling and by the look of it, gifts of flowers had already begun arriving for some lucky recipients.

Toni wasn't expecting any flowers or chocolates. Not even a card. She didn't have a special man in her life. Hadn't for ages. But she could still dream. Dream that someday she'd meet *the one*.

'Hi, stranger!' Liz Carey, Toni's senior counterpart and close friend greeted her.

Toni's soft laughter rippled. 'It's only been a week.'

'Nice break, though?' Liz's hands spanned her coffee mug.

'Sydney's always fabulous. Spent lots of time on the beach.'

'Mmm, I can see that,' Liz deadpanned. 'Love the tan.'

'Oh, ha.' Toni took the comment as lightly as it was meant. With her auburn hair and fair skin she had about as much chance of acquiring a tan as representing Australia at the Nationals. 'How have things been here?'

'Fairly OK.'

'New reg?'

Liz shrugged. 'Earning his keep.'

'And?' Toni's voice rose a notch.

'And nothing,' Liz shook her head. 'He seems professional. Made it his business to do the rounds of the shifts early on. Had a coffee with us—well, he had a green tea. Said he wanted to get to know us all asap. Amy Chan's back, by the way.'

'Oh…' Toni's eyes softened. 'How is she?'

'Ask her yourself,' Liz said. 'Here she is.'

'Ames!' Toni dropped her bag on to a nearby table and swooped the younger woman into a hug. 'How are you?'

'I'm good, Toni.' Amy shook back her bob of shiny black hair and smiled.

'Really?'

'Really,' Amy affirmed softly.

'And Leo?'

'He's fine. And thanks from both of us for—well, everything.'

'Hey, no problem.' Toni waved the other's thanks away. As nurse manager, she regarded her team almost as family. 'And anything you need, little break here and there, just ask, all right?'

The young nurse nodded and then turned as Justin Lawrence, one of their junior resident doctors, stuck his head in and called, 'Amy, these just came for you.' He held up a ceramic pot of bright red gerberas swathed in scarlet ribbons.

'For me…?' Amy put a hand to her heart and blushed prettily. 'They'll be from Leo.' She took off to collect her flowers as though her feet had wings.

'Leo's such a nice husband,' Liz said.

'Mmm.' Toni's gaze was faintly wistful. 'Red in the Chinese culture is the symbol for good luck, isn't it?'

'Something like that. Heaven knows, they could do with a bit.'

'Now, about the reg,' Toni persisted, tugging Liz aside. 'What are you not telling me?'

Liz rolled her eyes. 'You're like a dog with a damn great bone. It was a rotten week, stretched all of us. Riccardi was…tetchy.'

Toni frowned. 'With the staff?' She considered her team extremely well trained.

'With life in general, I think. There was an accident at that demolition job on Linton Road. A beam fell on a young apprentice. He…died.'

'Oh, lord.' Toni squeezed her eyes shut for a second. 'Was Riccardi called to the scene?'

Liz nodded. 'And that happened on Monday so it rather set the tone for the rest of the week.'

Toni looked thoughtful. Rotten days happened in A and E. That was the nature of the department. As a senior doctor, Riccardi should know how to hack it. And if he couldn't, why on earth had he taken the job? She was still holding the puzzling thought when the man himself strode in. *Oh, wow…* Toni's breath lodged and then came out slowly. He *was* as tall as she remembered. Taller, tougher, masculine to his fingertips. And his eyes, the shade of an early morning ocean, a kind of wintergreen, were tracking over her.

'Antonia.' He gave a formal little nod. 'Nice to see you back.'

And that, decided Toni, was where his effort to be polite stopped.

'Could someone turn that racket off?' he growled, making his way to the electric urn. He selected a tea bag from a canister and slammed it into a mug. 'Now,' he said levelly as he waited for his mug to fill with boiling water.

Ed, one of the junior nurses, obliged and the Beatles' version of *All you need is love* was strangled. 'It's Valentine's Day, Doc,' he protested with a laugh. 'You need to get in the zone.'

Riccardi's underbrowed look said, *Are you for real?*

'We'll all be going to the dance at the workers' club tonight.' Amy smiled, holding onto her little pot of flowers tightly. 'You must come, Dr Riccardi.'

The registrar snorted. 'I'd rather cut off my own feet.' He dangled his tea bag briefly and then discarded it in the bin. 'Without anaesthetic,' he added for good measure, before he strode out.

Liz sighed. 'Well, that went down well. Poor Amy. That was a bit unnecessary, wasn't it?'

'Yes.' Toni felt her temper fray. She'd seen Amy's expression falter; she'd bitten her lip and looked as though she hadn't known whether to laugh or cry. For heaven's sake, she was only trying to be friendly. She certainly hadn't deserved to cop the brunt of Riccardi's foul mood. Well, she wasn't having it! 'Lizzie, take handover, please? I need to sort this.'

Watching her friend take off out of the room, Liz muttered, 'Oh, you're for it, Riccardi.' When it came to standing up for her team, Toni was like a lioness defending her cubs.

'Dr Riccardi?' Toni raised her voice, moving along the corridor with the speed of light. She caught up with the registrar outside his office. 'I'd like a word, please?'

'It's Rafe,' he said shortly. 'Is there a problem?'

'Yes.' Toni sucked in her breath. 'Your attitude.'

One dark eyebrow arched and her less than diplomatic statement hung in the air between them. 'You'd better come in, then.'

'No, thanks.' Toni shook her head. She didn't want to

go into his office. She just wanted to state her case and get on with her day. 'I need time for a coffee before I start my shift.'

'I have coffee.' He flicked a hand towards his open office door.

Toni floundered for a second and then thought, Oh, what the heck. And followed him in.

He indicated the cafetière on the bench table near the window. 'Maureen still insists on providing fresh coffee every morning as she did for Joe, even though I've told her it's not necessary.'

Toni bit the edge of her lip through a reluctant smile. Maureen O'Dea had been Joe Lyons's secretary for ever and definitely wasn't about to be told to change her longstanding protocol. 'You don't drink coffee at all, then?'

'Not much. Help yourself,' he invited.

Toni did, drawing in the aroma of freshly brewed coffee as she poured. It was much nicer than the instant in the staffroom and she guessed she should be grateful for what was supposedly a small peace offering from Rafe Riccardi. But she wasn't about to be sidetracked from her mission.

'Have a seat,' he offered.

Nursing her mug of coffee, Toni slipped into the chair, facing him across his desk. 'I don't want this to be confrontational.'

'OK.' He raised his mug and took a mouthful of his tea and studied her in silence for a second, then his mouth quirked. 'I won't bite. So, speak to me, Antonia.'

Toni took a deep breath and straightened her shoulders. 'I'm usually called Toni.'

'Pity.' His stormy green gaze tangled with hers. 'Antonia is a beautiful name.'

Well, it was the way *he* said it, low and expressive and newly awake, early-morning sexy. And it completely trashed her defences. She regrouped jerkily. She had to say what she'd come to say. 'Amy Chan is just getting over losing a baby at twenty weeks.'

A beat of silence.

'And I need to know this because…?' Riccardi leaned back in his chair and waited.

'Because your response when she invited you to the Valentine's party was offhand. In fact, it was bordering on rude. You embarrassed her and she's only just returned to work—she's still fragile. If we're to work successfully as a team, we need mutual respect and at least a show of good manners.'

Suddenly the silence was as thick as custard. Toni tightened her fingers around her coffee mug. Had she gone too far? As the senior medical officer for the department, Rafe Riccardi's toes were definitely not for treading on. 'I realise you're new to the place and getting to know everyone takes time…' She stopped and wished she could dive under the desk and hide from his penetrating green gaze. But there was no chance of that.

'Fine, then.' A contained little smile played around his mouth. 'You've made your point. I'll straighten things out with Amy and with the department in general.'

'And show your face at the Valentine dance?' Toni jumped in where a lesser person would have feared to tread.

His jaw tensed. 'You don't give up, do you? What's all the hype about St Valentine's Day anyway? It's for lovers, isn't it? Then let the lovers of the world get on with it.'

Toni dropped her gaze. This was the oddest kind of conversation to be having with a man she'd only known for five minutes. She took a mouthful of her coffee and tried to marshal her thoughts. 'I realise for some people Valentine's Day is a pain but for the others it's loaded with romance.'

He snorted.

'Well, it is!' Toni emphasised.

'It's commercialism at its worst.'

'OK.' Toni batted a hand in a kind of aggrieved acceptance. 'We've established you're not into it. But here at
Forrestdale St Valentine's Day is always set aside for the
big fundraiser of the year. This year's project is a state-of-
the-art ultrasound. It will be mainly in use in Midwifery.'
Toni paused. *If they'd had better scanning equipment for
Amy...* But that wasn't the problem. As Amy's Ob, Hannah
Gordon, had assured the couple, the baby had just been
too early, not viable. Toni blinked a bit. 'Anyway, that's
about it. Tonight's dinner-dance is about raising funds.'

'I'll give a donation,' Rafe said flatly. And he'd make
it a hefty one. Anonymously, of course.

'Up to you.' Toni got to her feet. There'd been a glim-
mer of hope she could have talked him round. She may as
well have saved her breath. She placed her mug back on
the side table. 'I guess we'll catch up sooner rather than
later, then. Mondays are usually a bit full on.'

And then she turned and he caught the full force of
her smile. It was so warm, so natural, as if she did it a lot.
Smiled, that was. He stood courteously as she left, his
breath jamming in his throat.

Antonia Morell was one sassy lady. He sank back into
his chair feeling a bit dazed. He'd actually enjoyed spar-
ring with her. And that incredible auburn hair... The way
she wore it, wild and untamed, had to say so much about
her personality. Out of nowhere, he imagined her on a
speedboat on Sydney Harbour, cutting through the spray,
her hair windblown, crazy curls all over the place streaming out behind her. Or snugly tamed inside a snow beanie
with just some bright tendrils poking out. Or softly shiny
spread on a pillow...

Hell. He yanked his X-rated thoughts to a halt. Get a grip Riccardi. You're not on the prowl here, no matter how tempting the prize. You're on a timeline. Three months to be exact. So, just keep your head down and do your job and at the end of your contract you can show those boffins on the medical board you're fit and able to get back in the field.

Toni's thoughts were mixed as she made her way back to the nurses' station. Rafe Riccardi baffled her. Intrigued her. Self-contained. A bit of a loner. Could be nicer if he tried a bit harder. Oh, for heaven's sake. She made a little sound of dismissal. She wasn't giving him a school report.

One glance told her the department was already busy. Liz put down the phone and looked up, her well-shaped brows raised in query. 'Is he still in one piece?'

'Of course.' Toni began slotting pens into her top pocket. 'We got engaged.'

Liz smothered a squawk and then chuckled. 'We've missed you.'

'Yeah.' Toni shook back her halo of auburn curls. 'Now, who's doing what?'

'Justin's suturing in the small treatment room. Beryl Reilly took a dive down the post-office steps this morning. Kneecap nearly split in two.'

Toni grimaced. 'Poor old love.' Beryl, in her seventies, was one of their regulars at A and E. 'Why on earth was she out and about so early?'

'Posting coupons for some cruise or other. Today was the last day to enter apparently.'

'Oh, my lord,' Toni sighed. 'What would she do if she won? She'd never go on her own.'

Liz snickered. 'She'd probably hook up with one of the old guys from their indoor bowls team and take him along.'

'We shouldn't laugh.' Toni pressed a finger to her smiling lips. 'It's very sweet, really, the way they all look out for each other.'

'And Beryl probably has about as much chance of winning as we do of getting a raise.'

'OK, back to business,' Toni said firmly. 'Who's assisting Justin?'

'Harmony. Not that she wanted to,' Liz added caustically. 'She hates anything to do with blood.'

'Well, she's only newly graduated,' Toni reasoned. 'These days they're not exposed to much on the wards in their training. It's always a bit of shock when they strike the real thing. Where's Ed?'

'Doing an eye-wash. One of the council workers copped a load of sand and grit when they were unloading turf for the new sports oval.'

Toni nodded. 'Amy OK?'

'I've assigned her to tidy the drugs cabinet with Mel. The night shift left a tip.'

'Well, they had two RTAs in quick succession, by the look of it.' Toni scanned the report. 'This one says Riccardi was the admitting MO.'

'So?'

'So that means he's been here since four o'clock this morning.' Toni made a small face. 'No wonder he was grouchy. The man's missing sleep.'

'It's his job.' Liz was not so forgiving. 'It's what he signed on for.'

'I wonder what he was doing before coming here?' Toni mused.

'Dunno. Don't tell me you're falling for him?'

'As if,' Toni responded with a little tsk. 'Perhaps we should cut him a bit of slack, though. Forrestdale might be a huge lifestyle change for him.'

'Well, there's usually a trigger for those kinds of decisions,' Liz pointed out pragmatically. 'But I'm for making love, not war, so we'll be nice to your reg.'

'He's not *my* reg,' Toni said in exasperation. 'Now, both Natalie and Samantha in?' she asked, referring to the department's assistants in nursing.

'By the grace of God. And Dr Tennant is circulating if we need her.'

'Excellent.' Toni clipped on her badge and checked it was straight. 'I'll ask her to pop in on our eye patient. He may need an antibiotic and a medical certificate for work.'

'Uh-oh,' Liz sighed as their phone lit up. 'Call from the ambulance base. Welcome to Monday!'

Toni took the details from Liz. 'Mine, I think, and I'll bleep the reg.'

They met at the ambulance bay and Toni relayed what details they had. 'Unrestrained two-year-old thrown against the dashboard when his mum had to brake suddenly. He appears to have been knocked out for a second but conscious now.'

'The child was in the front seat of the car?' Rafe asked in disbelief.

'Apparently.' Toni twitched a shoulder. 'We don't know the circumstances. It may not be the mother's fault.'

'Well, we certainly can't blame the child,' Rafe said grimly. 'Do we have names?'

'Child is Michael. Mum is Lisa.'

He received the information with a curt nod. He'd have a few words to say to *Lisa*. Having a child unrestrained in a moving vehicle was totally irresponsible.

The ambulance arrived and reversed into the receiving bay. One glance told Toni the mother was distraught. 'It's all my fault!' Lisa was all but wringing her hands. 'The childminder is only two streets away and I was running late so I just popped him in the front seat beside me—but he's learned how to undo the seat belt—' She broke off, rubbing tears away with the backs of her hands. She sent a frantic look at Rafe. 'Will I be in trouble? What will happen now?'

Despite his earlier silent disapproval at the mother's negligence, Rafe's heart melted at the sight of the little lad lying quietly under the blue blanket, his eyes wide and questioning.

His mouth tightened. There were extenuating circumstances and he didn't have the stomach for a confrontation anyway. Not today. And especially not with Antonia watching his every reaction with those soulful brown eyes. He regrouped his thoughts.

'We'll take a look at Michael,' he said gruffly. 'Try not to worry. Children are remarkably resilient.'

'Can I stay with him?'

Toni jumped in, 'Of course you can.'

'Oh—thank you.' Lisa held tightly to her child's hand as he was whisked through into a cubicle.

'Lisa, if you could just stand back, please?' Toni eased the mother away from the side of the bed. 'Dr Riccardi will need room to examine Michael.'

Still visibly shaken, Lisa complied, wrapping her arms around her body almost as if she could hold herself together in some way. 'I'm here, baby,' she said brokenly. 'Mummy's just here…'

The child looked clean and well cared for, Toni noted, peeling the blanket back gently. 'Doctor?' She looked pointedly at Rafe.

'Thanks.' Rafe began his examination. 'Let's see how you're doing, little mate,' he said, his hands gentle, swift and sure as he tested the child's neurological responses. 'Looking good,' he murmured, as Michael's pupils appeared equal and responsive. Placing his pencil torch aside, he checked the little boy's limbs for any obvious deficits and then began a careful palpation of the child's tummy. Any hardening would indicate internal bleeding. But all seemed well. He replaced the blanket and turned to the mother.

'Was he sick at all, Lisa?'

'No.' She shook her head. 'He just seemed out of it for a second or two and then cried a bit...'

Rafe nodded. 'I'd like to run a scan to be on the safe side. And we'll need to keep your son for several hours, just to make sure there are no residual effects from the accident.'

'It really *was* an accident.' Lisa stood her ground bravely. 'This guy just shot out of his driveway without warning and I had to slam on my brakes. I realise I should have had Michael in the back in his safety seat.'

'But you didn't.' Rafe continued writing on the child's chart.

'I was going after a new job,' Lisa explained dispiritedly. 'But I've lost my interview time now.'

'There'll be other jobs.' Absorbed in Michael's chart, Rafe curled his lips into a silent no-further-comment moue. He handed the request form for the X-ray department to Toni. 'After Michael's scan could you see whether Kids could take him, please? He'll be more comfortable there. And ask Justin to check Lisa over and perhaps we could run to a coffee for her?'

Toni gave him a taut little smile. 'I'm sure we could.'

Rafe pulled back the curtain to make his exit and then wheeled back, the light from the window illuminating the hard line of his jaw with its rapidly darkening growth. 'I'd like to see the X-rays when they're back, please, Antonia?'

'Certainly, Doctor.' Toni's response was crisply calm

but a niggle of uncertainty caught her unawares. She'd told Riccardi she was usually called *Toni*. Why couldn't he just do it? Perhaps it was as simple as his not liking shortened names. She frowned a bit. Whatever his reasons, it was already setting her apart and causing the oddest trickle of awareness along her spine.

CHAPTER TWO

BACK in his office, Rafe threw aside the medical journal he'd been reading.

It may as well have been written in a foreign language for all he'd taken in.

Antonia Morell. The cameo-like picture was still there in his head. Her complexion magnolia fair against the dazzling auburn hair; the quick, intelligent air about her. And the amazing smile that outlined the sweet curve of her mouth. Her mouth...

Disconcerted, he rubbed a hand across his cheekbones. The wild feelings of want were annoying him, disturbing him. He didn't need them. He just needed to get through the next few months, recoup his energy, regain his enthusiasm...

'Rafe...?' Toni popped her head around the door. He looked up and she saw at once she'd interrupted a very focused train of thought. 'Sorry...the door was open...'

'Come in, Antonia.' He voice was slightly rough. 'What's up?'

'You said you wanted to see Michael's CT scan.' Toni moved towards his desk, feeling as though she was walking in sand, ankle deep. 'He's up in Kids now. Amy asked to special him.'

Rafe's dark brows rose interrogatively. 'Is that wise?'

Toni bristled at his implied criticism. 'Are you saying I should be keeping her away from babies and toddlers?'

'No.' He glinted an impatient green glance at her. 'You mentioned she's a bit fragile at the moment, that's all.'

'It was her decision.' Toni placed the large envelope on the desk in front of him. 'In fact, she said she hoped we wouldn't think we had to keep walking on eggshells around her.'

'Well, that sounds positive.' Spinning off his chair, Rafe selected the first plate and slapped it on to the viewing screen. 'I'll need a word with Lisa,' he murmured almost absently. 'Ask her to pop in and see me when you have a minute.'

'Uh…' Toni hesitated. 'She's actually not in the hospital just now.'

'She's gone?' Rafe's dark head swooped back in question. 'She's left her boy here and just gone off somewhere? Where are the woman's priorities?' He put the next plate up and studied it. 'The whole trauma for this child is down to his mother's failure to carry out the basic safety rules for young children in cars.'

'You're putting the wrong spin on it,' Toni said heatedly and went on to explain, 'Lisa had a phone call. Apparently, she managed to reschedule her job interview. She's a sole parent, Rafe. She needs a full-time job not just the bits and pieces she presently has. You saw how upset she was about Michael's accident. She doesn't need you jumping all over her as well.'

'You're breaking my heart, Antonia,' he growled, clearly unimpressed with Toni's defence of the young mother.

'And which *heart* would that be, exactly?' she inquired tartly.

The corners of his mouth pulled down almost comically. 'I've really rained on your parade today, haven't I?'

Toni rolled her eyes heavenwards. Really, the man was impossible.

'This all looks good.' He drew her attention to the last of the X-rays. 'Michael has been fortunate.'

'He's sporting quite a lump on his forehead, though.' Toni positioned herself beside Rafe and looked at the screen.

'I'll write up some pain relief for him. That whack has possibly left the little guy with a headache. And let's keep the neuro obs going, please? I'm not letting him go until I'm quite sure he's stable.'

'All noted.' Toni swept out.

She made her way back to the nurses' station, the busyness of the morning enveloping her. But an hour later, she was on her way upstairs to the children's ward. Amy needed a break.

She popped her head in, turning to speak to Jennifer on the desk. 'Michael Yates, Jen?'

The senior nurse flapped a hand. 'Right down the end in the cot. The reg arrived a while ago to check him over. He's gorgeous, isn't he?'

'Michael?'

Jennifer rolled her eyes. 'Riccardi.'

Toni wasn't about to go there. She still hadn't made up her mind about anything to do with Rafe Riccardi. 'He probably is,' she flannelled instead. 'If you go for tall, dark, bloody-minded men.'

'Oh, my stars, Toni Morell!' A teasing smile curved Jen's mouth. 'You fancy him!'

Toni clicked her tongue exasperatedly and skipped away, drawing to an abrupt stop when she saw Rafe and Amy, their heads together in obvious earnest conversation. She watched as Amy's dark little head came back and she laughed at something Rafe said. And then he touched the nurse briefly on the shoulder before exiting from the door at the far end of the ward.

'Well, ten out of ten,' Toni murmured, feeling a tiny flicker of satisfaction. Rafe had obviously taken their talk to heart and made the effort to smooth things over with Amy. He'd kept his word. And that, as far as Toni was concerned, had earned him a large tick of approval.

Oh, heck! Impatiently, she swept her hair up from the nape of her neck and let it fall back. Surely she wasn't actually beginning to *like* the man?

She walked briskly along the ward to Michael's cot. 'Everything OK?' she asked softly.

'Still a bit out of it, I think.' Amy was sitting by the cot, stroking the toddler's chubby little arm.

'That's understandable.' Toni ran her eye over the chart. Pain relief had been administered and the child was being kept hydrated. There was little more they could do now than to monitor Michael's neuro responses. If nothing untoward presented, Rafe would probably allow Lisa to take her son home. 'He'll probably drop off to sleep soon.' Toni bent and touched a finger to the baby-soft cheek. 'But, Amy, if for any reason you have to take him out of the cot, be sure to carry him, won't you? We don't want him falling.'

'I *have* nursed in Kids before, Toni,' Amy said with a wry little smile. 'I'll take great care of Michael.'

'Of course you will.' Toni made a face. 'Sorry. I'm a bit distracted this morning.'

Amy chuckled. 'The new reg would distract anyone.'

Toni held back a cryptic comment. Not Amy too. 'Mel is coming up to relieve you shortly. It's time for your break. Make sure you take it, please.'

There was a flurry around the station when Toni returned to Casualty. 'What's going on?'

'These amazing roses just arrived!' Harmony's blonde ponytail jiggled as her head tipped from side to side in excitement.

Toni's heart almost juddered to a stop. Surely he hadn't…? She looked helplessly at the blooms in the florist's basket, with the chirpy little red hearts dancing from the wicker handle. Oh, lord… There had to be dozens of roses, all colours, and the perfume was divine.

'They're old-fashioned garden roses,' Liz said knowledgeably. 'My granddad grows beauties like these. They must have cost a fortune.'

'Who are they for?' Toni hoped no one but her could hear the little catch in her voice.

'Apparently, they're for the whole staff of the A and E.' Liz held out the card. 'See?'

Oh, for heaven's sake. Toni stifled a groan. It seemed as though Riccardi was tearing around like a head stockman, mending fences all over the place.

'Someone must think we're pretty, damned hot,' Ed joked. 'The dream team!' He did a high five with Harmony.

'Could be from the Mayor,' Justin said. 'Remember, Joe operated on that infected ingrown toenail just before he left on leave?'

Liz snorted. 'Bit of an extravagant thank you for an ingrown toenail! Toni.' She turned to her friend. 'Any ideas?'

Plenty, Toni thought, her heart returning slowly to its rightful place. But none she could voice here. 'Perhaps, we'll never know.' She sidestepped the question deftly. 'But we should get them in water for a start.' She turned to one of their AINs. 'Job for you, Sam?'

'But there are heaps!' The youngster looked dismayed. 'What shall I do with them all?'

'We could send some up to Midwifery,' Toni suggested.

'No,' Liz dismissed. 'They always have plenty.'

'I'm about to take my break,' Ed said cheerfully. 'Why don't I bike some over to the aged-care home? Give the oldies a buzz?'

'*Seniors*, Ed,' Toni reminded him, and then gave one of her megawatt smiles. 'But I think that's a wonderful idea. Are we all agreed?'

There was a chorus of approval.

'The roses were from *him,* weren't they?' Liz demanded, when she and Toni had a minute on their own.

'Probably.' Toni had given up the fight to try to remain neutral.

'The atmosphere in the place has lightened a hundred per cent since the flowers arrived,' Liz said. 'What on earth did you say to him?'

'Probably far too much.' But he'd given back as much as he'd got. In fact, they'd matched strikes like a couple of jousting combatants. Toni smothered a reminiscent smile. She'd enjoyed it, jousting with Rafe Riccardi. She wondered if he'd felt the same…

'But it was such a nice gesture!' Liz shook her head in quiet amazement. 'You must have worked a small miracle on His Grumpiness.' She chuckled.

'I'm sure Rafe will be more sociable when he's caught up on sleep,' Toni responded, and wondered why she was going to bat for him. 'Are you coming to the dinner do?' She changed conversation lanes deftly.

'You bet. It's the first night out we've had in weeks. Mum is babysitting Lulu and William, and Matt's promised to leave the studios early. Or I'll kill him,' Liz added calmly.

Toni smiled. Liz's husband worked as a producer at the local radio station. 'You're so lucky, Lizzie. Two sweet kids and a husband who comes home to you at night.'

Liz rolled her eyes. 'What about you? Are you bringing someone?'

'No.' Toni was definite. 'I aim to stay for the dinner and then take off.'

'Not staying for the slow dancing?' Liz waggled her brows suggestively.

'That's all right for young lovers and you old married folk,' Toni dismissed. 'If I want to get up close and personal with a bloke, I'd rather challenge him to a game of tennis.'

Liz flipped some files into an out-tray. 'You're such a romantic!'

Toni showed Liz the tip of her tongue. 'You'd be surprised what you can learn about someone's character in a sporting context—especially if they're losing. I believe the tickets have sold really well. Half the town seems to be going along.'

'Well, the raffle prizes are exceptional,' Liz said chattily. 'A couple of the motor dealers have combined and donated a new car. And the winery's putting up six cases of their finest. The council's come good as well and contributed a luxury weekend for two at the Gold Coast.'

'Then let's hope folk are feeling generous and buy zillions of tickets,' Toni endorsed. 'That way we might just make enough to get our scanner.'

'It's quiet at the moment.' Liz checked the department with a practised eye. 'Mind if I take the early lunch? I want to get a shampoo and blow-wave.'

'Go.' Toni flapped a hand. 'And thanks for jinxing us. I bet every man and his dog will come trailing in now.'

'Well, you'll cope with the men.' Liz chuckled. 'Just send the dogs along to the vet. See you.' She grabbed her bag and took off.

Toni leaned on the counter, allowing herself a few moments of respite. Through the big plate-glass doors at the entrance she could see the gardens the groundsman, Kenny, had such pride in. In Australia, February was the hottest month on the calendar, yet he managed to nurture the plants along and now there were riotous splashes of colour everywhere.

Toni thought on. She was glad she lived in a country town in so many ways. But what was Rafe doing here? she wondered. And would they ever get close enough for him to confide in her?

Beside Toni, the emergency phone rang, bringing her back to reality with a snap. Replacing the receiver a few seconds later, she took off at speed towards Rafe's office. She hoped he was there.

He was, looking up in query as she popped her head in.

'Possible arrest coming into Resus. ETA six minutes.'

He was on his feet immediately and they were moving swiftly to the resus area. 'Do we have a name?' he asked.

'It's Carol McKay. She manages the dress shop in town. Cardiac history. The paramedics have given anginine with nil effect.'

'We'll have to wing it, then.' Rafe's voice was clipped. 'And hope we come up with the right answers. What about family? Anyone to be notified?'

'She's a widow. Son works at the school. I'll chase it up.'

'Delegate to someone else,' Rafe was firm. 'I want you scrubbed and ready to catheterise. If our patient is overloaded, we don't have time to mess about. Harmony?' He rounded on the young RN. 'I want you involved here, please.'

Harmony's eyes went wide. 'Yes, Doctor.'

'And as soon as our patient hits the deck, I need the monitor leads on *pronto*.'

'If the patient arrests, you're number three, Harmony.'
Toni was scrubbing furiously.

'Three?' Harmony looked agitatedly from one to the
other.

'You'll write what drugs are being given on the white-
board,' Toni said calmly. 'And help with the IV fluids
where necessary. You'll be fine.' She sent out a brief en-
couraging smile to the nurse.

'Right.' Harmony seemed spurred on by Toni's confidence and began to get the intubation tray ready.

And then it was time for action.

The ambulance reversed into the bay, its doors already
opening.

'Be good, team.' Rafe's words snapped out and Carol
McKay was wheeled rapidly into Resus.

The paramedic relayed what treatment they'd given,
adding, 'She's not looking great, Doc.'

Rafe wasted no time in supposition. They had a life
to save here. His hands moved like lightning, securing a
tourniquet and IV in seconds. 'Give me sixty of Lasix,'
he barked. 'IDC in now, please, Toni. Let's make a dent
in that fluid.'

Toni's hands were deft and sure. In seconds the indwell-
ing catheter was in situ.

'Good work,' Rafe murmured, as the crippling fluid
began draining away. 'OK, let's clamp at eight hundred
mil. Sixty of Lasix, please.'

Harmony passed the dose. 'That's one-twenty so far,
Doctor.'

'Adjust the oxygen to full now, please. Carol?' Rafe
leaned closer to his patient. 'Can you hear me? You're in
hospital. Did you forget to take your medication today?'

Carol's eyes fluttered open. 'Mmm,' she murmured.
'Sorry…'

'That's OK,' Rafe spoke gently. 'So long as we know, we can treat you. Try to relax now and breathe into the mask. How's the BP doing, Antonia?'

'One-sixty over a hundred. Pulse a hundred and ten, resps thirty.'

Rafe acknowledged her call with a swift nod. So far so good but his gut feeling was telling him they weren't out of the woods yet.

Toni began to sponge Carol's forehead. She still looked very unwell, very clammy… Alarm ripped through Toni and automatically she felt for a pulse. Nothing. She hit the arrest button. There was a flurry outside and Justin appeared.

'Will you intubate, please, Justin?' Rafe was professional and calm. 'And I need adrenaline ten here.'

Harmony slapped the prepared dose into his hand.

'And another ten. Any pulse?'

'No.' Toni felt her nerves pull tightly.

'Let's defib, then, please.'

'Charging.' Toni's teeth clenched on her lower lip.

'All clear.' Rafe discharged the paddles.

All gazes swung to the monitor.

'Damn all…' Rafe spat the words from between clenched teeth. 'Let's go again. Clear.'

This time the trace bleeped, faded and then staggered into a rhythm. 'Yes…' Rafe's relief was controlled. 'We've got her. Thanks, everyone.'

'You did really well today, Harmony.' Toni was fulsome in her praise for the younger woman.

'Oh—thanks, Toni.' Harmony gave a pleased smile.

They were putting the resus room back to rights, Carol McKay having been transferred to the hospital's small IC unit. 'I've had a few doubts about working in A and E,' she confessed, stuffing the used linen into a laundry bin.

'Well, it's not for everyone,' Toni agreed. 'Is there an area you'd prefer?'

Harmony bit her lip. 'It's difficult to know when I've only just begun my nursing. We were sheltered from quite a bit in our training. It's different when you're actually part of the team.'

'Well, never be afraid to ask,' Toni counselled. 'You're newly graduated. You're not expected to know everything. I think we're about finished in here.' She did a quick inventory. 'Anything you want to debrief about before we go?'

Harmony hesitated. 'Will we be transferring Carol on?'

'Not at this stage. Rafe is presently calling her cardiologist in Sydney. We'll know a bit more later.'

'I…guess she won't be able to open her shop for a while?'

'Not sure,' Toni said. 'She may have someone who could stand in for her. Carol has great stock. Have you bought anything there?'

'I actually bought a dress for the Valentine dance.' Harmony made a small face. 'Carol was having it altered it for me. I was supposed to pick it up after work today.'

Toni was sympathetic to the younger woman's obvious disappointment. 'Have you something else you could wear?'

'Nothing new.' Harmony shrugged dispiritedly. 'I so wanted this dress, Toni.' Her cheeks went pink. 'Justin's asked me to go with him.'

Dating a doctor. Toni gave an inward wry smile. She'd done a bit of that in her time. And it had been fun—until she'd met Dr Alex Nicol. He'd come as a relieving MO to St Vincent's in Sydney, where she'd been working in A and E. And she'd fallen for him, beguiled by his Geordie accent, his craggy looks, his sense of humour. He'd told her he was separated and getting divorced and she'd believed him. But then it turned out, he hadn't been truthful…

Toni stifled the unproductive trip into past. It was water under the Harbour bridge. Gone. Like Alex had gone back to England. To his wife.

'Hey, guys.' Amy popped her head in. 'Need a hand to clear up?'

'We're about done, thanks, Amy.' Toni jerked back to the present, refolding the blanket she'd been holding.

'What's up?' Amy had caught her air of introspection. 'Carol will be all right, won't she?'

'Should be,' Toni said. 'But with Carol away from her shop, Harmony has a bit of a dilemma about her dress for tonight.'

Amy was all attention. 'What's happened, Harms?'

Harmony explained her difficulty.

'I could lend you something.' Amy gave the junior a quick assessing look. 'We're about the same size. And I got some amazing clothes recently when Leo and I were over in Singapore. Why don't we hook up after work and go back to mine? If you like something, it's yours. OK?'

'Are you kidding me?' Harmony's blue eyes widened in happy disbelief. 'That would so be totally awesome. I love your style, Amy!'

'Oh, thanks.' Harmony dimpled a smile. 'Deal, then?'

'Deal.'

Laughing, the two walked off together, heads turned towards each other, eagerly discussing the celebrations for the night ahead.

Toni smiled after them. It was good to see Amy so upbeat. Plus, professionally, she would be an excellent role model for Harmony.

Nice outcome. Somewhat thoughtfully, Toni made her

way back to the station. There were good vibes all over the place. Had it all happened because of an armful of roses?

She wondered whether Rafe realised just what effect his gesture had achieved—if indeed the roses had been from him. But of course they had to have been…

And it was a bit daunting to think he'd been spurred into action because of something she'd said.

She wasn't about to ask him.

But he *had* to know that she knew.

So where did they go from here?

Toni puffed out a little breath to stem her consternation. Her heartbeat kicked up a notch. She hadn't expected this complication on her first day back. Correction. She hadn't expected it at all.

The afternoon ticked by. A few mild casualties trickled in that were handled competently by Justin and the nursing staff.

Liz had arrived back from the hairdresser, her hair sleek and shiny with little tendrils curling prettily from a loose knot.

'Hair looks great,' Toni said approvingly.

Liz sighed. 'Wish I'd had time for a spray tan.'

'Matt likes you just the way you are.' Toni tipped her head enquiringly. 'And the spark's still there, isn't it?'

Liz smiled mistily. 'Oh, yeah…'

'Well, then.' Toni glanced at the clock on the wall. It was almost the end of their working day. 'Lizzie, will you hand over, please? I need to see Rafe about a few things before end of shift.'

'Sure. See you tonight?'

'If you're there first, keep me a seat.'

Liz grinned wickedly. 'I'll keep two. You never know!'

Ten minutes later, Toni tapped on Rafe's door and waited. Her eyes went heavenwards at his growled response, '*It's open.*' Suddenly her heart felt as though it was beating in all the wrong places in her chest. Had this been a crazy idea? Well, it was too late now.

Angling herself through the door, she moved across to his desk. 'I pushed the boat out and got us an energy hit from the canteen.' She passed the disposable cup across to him. 'Hot chocolate for you, coffee for me.'

He eyed her a bit warily, seeming surprised and even a bit taken aback, and Toni wondered how long it had been since anyone had done a simple act of kindness for him. 'Thanks. How did you know I needed this?'

'Put it down to my powers of observation.' Toni slid into the same chair she'd occupied that morning. Cradling her coffee between her hands, she asked, 'What's happening with Carol McKay?'

Rafe tilted his cup and took a mouthful of his hot chocolate. Seeming to enjoy it, he took another. 'I had a video hook-up with her cardiologist. He's of the opinion if there's no further deterioration in her condition, she can be safely managed here.'

'That should be less stressful for her anyway,' Toni replied. 'She can keep up with things at her business. Carol has quite a large customer base, most of whom have become her friends. They'll be concerned for her welfare.'

'Her son's with her now in ICU. I imagine he'll help her work out some kind of plan for the future.'

'I expect so. She won't want to lose trade if it's at all possible.'

'That's not likely, is it?'

'Probably not.' Toni sipped her coffee. 'It's the only decent dress shop in town so where else are the ladies going to go?'

'I have no idea, Antonia.' A tiny flicker of amusement appeared behind Rafe's eyes. 'Online perhaps?'

'Don't think so,' Toni drawled, a hint of laughter edging her voice. 'Online shopping hasn't hit Forrestdale to any great degree. As for the girls, they're more inclined to want to *touch* before they buy, rather than just visualise it on a screen.'

'Interesting.' He gave a guarded kind of smile that rapidly spun out to lighten his whole face. He had no idea what they were talking about but Toni smiled right back and their smiles dallied for a moment, then caught and held. And suddenly his office was full of something neither of them understood.

Toni drew back in her chair. Her body felt tingly with electricity. Odd. And Rafe's laughing eyes were warming her from head to toe. Oh, boy, oh, boy... This could get complicated. And she needed *that* like a tax bill.

In a split second Rafe decided he didn't need whatever it was that was happening here. Were they flirting? Hell, this was a minefield. Silence permeated the atmosphere and in order to break it he swivelled his chair slightly so that he was looking through the window at the patchwork of distant gum trees, blue summer sky and high cloud. He took a deep breath to steady himself and then glanced pointedly at his watch. 'You'd better take off, hadn't you— if you're going out tonight?'

Toni looked startled. Was he dismissing her? It sure seemed like it. She swallowed the last mouthful of her coffee and rose to her feet. 'Why don't you take an early mark as well?' she said lightly. 'You look bushed.'

'Do I?' he replied blandly.

'Yes.' She'd already noticed the charcoal shadows beneath his eyes and the way he'd rolled back his shoulders out on the ward as if trying to stave off a bone-crunching weariness. 'Go home, Rafe.'

'Hey!' Rafe planted his feet and uncurled to his full height 'Who's the boss here?'

'You, Dr Riccardi,' Toni returned sweetly. 'But surely you know how to delegate? There's a competent late shift already on duty and I'm sure they'll call you in if anything unmanageable occurs.'

Rafe stifled a hoot of raw laughter. The only thing unmanageable was Antonia Morell. But she was right. He was whacked. 'OK, you win.' He gave in, dragging his hands through his hair and locking them at the back of his neck.

'I'll take off.'

'Have a good night, then. Although…' Toni paused with her hand on the doorknob and shot him one of her smiles '…if you feel like it later, you could pop over to the dance and draw one of the raffle prizes for us.'

Rafe let out a breath of pure relief as he watched her neat little backside disappear out the door. But she'd left in her wake a whole chain of emotions that gnawed at his insides. He'd wanted this post in Forrestdale to be as straightforward as possible. No bumps in the road. No emotional involvement to leave behind. And now all that seemed turned on its head.

But only if he let it…

He whipped his medical case out of its locker. He needed to breathe in some fresh air, even swim fifty laps of the pool if that's what it took to get his head on straight again.

Had she really done that in there? A long breath jagged its way from Toni's lungs. Surely she hadn't batted her eyelashes at him, had she? But she'd certainly been *flirty*. Perhaps he hadn't noticed? But of course he had—he'd done it right back at her. Were they game-playing? Toni shook her head. She didn't do games. Ever. Then what on earth had got into her just now?

She fled to the staffroom. Hauling her bag out of the locker, she headed for the car park. Good grief! Why was she letting herself get tied in knots like this? And over a man again. A man who was here today and gone tomorrow—well, in three months' time. And she'd been down that road. Heck, she'd scrubbed the kitchen floor with one of his T-shirts!

As she slowed to accommodate the after-school traffic flow, Toni released a long calming breath. She needed something physical to unleash the frustration that was robbing her of plain common sense. She felt like thrashing someone at tennis but her club didn't meet until Thursday evening. Well, she'd just have to run. Run and run. And hope by the end of it she'd be restored to her usual level-headed thinking.

CHAPTER THREE

TONI pushed herself, running lap after lap around the track adjacent to the park. Then, deciding she'd had enough, she leaned forward, hands on the fence railings, warming down. She jogged home leisurely, deciding she'd left herself just enough time to get ready for the Valentine party.

Showered, she blotted her hair dry and then stepped into her favourite silk underwear. She'd bought new clothes on her recent trip to Sydney. Now she just had to decide what to wear. And these days she pleased herself.

After flicking through her choices, she decided to dress simply in a sleeveless silk dress with a crossover bodice. In a dusky blush pink, it had a short draped skirt that fell just above her knees. She puffed perfume into the air and walked through it, then reached for the dress and slid it over her head.

Her make-up was minimal as usual— -a touch of tinted moisturiser on her cheeks, a flick of muted shadow on her lids and lipstick in a soft coral. She slipped her feet into high-heeled sandals, pushed a broad silver bangle on her arm and stood back to get the overall picture in the mirror. The dress was gorgeous, the faint shimmer in the material pearling the fairness of her skin and highlighting her hair.

She'd do.

Toni drove across to the club. She intended to have

only one glass of wine to celebrate and then she'd stay with mineral water. Besides, the evening was too warm to drink alcohol. But that wouldn't stop most of the guests, she thought realistically.

She managed to park near the entrance of the club, which would be good for her early exit, she thought, sliding out of her car and activating the locking device on her keypad.

'Toni!' Hearing her name, Toni spun round to see Liz and Matt getting out of a taxi. She fluttered a wave and waited for them to catch up. 'You look terrific, Lizzie,' she said with a smile. Liz was wearing a bold red gown that floated to her ankles.

'Thanks, I think.' Liz looked doubtful. 'It's not too…?' She indicated the deep cleavage.

'It's gorgeous,' Toni reassured her. 'If you've got it, flaunt it!'

'That's what I told her.' Matt stuffed his wallet into his back pocket after paying off the cabbie. 'How are you, Tone?' He placed a peck on her cheek.

'I'm fine, thanks, Matt. It should be a good night.'

Chatting, they made their way inside to the club's function room.

'Doesn't everything look spectacular?' Toni gave a little cry of delight, casting her eyes around at the table settings with their crisp white cloths and tea-lights. The mandatory hearts and roses were everywhere, although Toni doubted the roses were real. Unlike the beauties they'd received at the hospital…

'Oh, here are some of our gang now,' Liz said as Amy and Harmony arrived with their respective partners.

'The girls look so pretty.' Toni smiled. Both were wearing soft, floaty florals.

'At their age, it would be a crime not to,' Liz responded dryly. 'This seems to be our table here.'

'I'll get some drinks,' Matt said. 'Toni, white wine?'

Toni nodded. 'Thanks, Matt.'

'You look amazing, by the way,' Liz said as they took their places at the big round table. 'Sydney?'

'My favourite dress shop in Rose Bay.'

'Shame Rafe's not coming.'

'Actually, he seemed pretty tired.'

'Still,' Liz contended, 'it would have been a good look for the department if he'd shown.'

Toni raised a shoulder stiffly. Well, she'd asked him and he wasn't here. But she was keeping that information strictly to herself.

The Valentine fundraiser would be a success, Toni decided as the evening wore on. Folk were in a happy and giving mood and tickets for their raffle were practically sold out. And the supper set out in buffet-style had been exceptional. And now people were beginning to drift on to the dance-floor.

Their table had emptied almost as soon as the dance music had begun. Left on her own, Toni took off towards the powder room, deciding she'd stay until they'd drawn the raffle and then she'd be away to her bed.

After refreshing her lipstick, Toni left the powder room. As she passed the bar on the way back to the table, she stopped and almost froze. Rafe was standing with his hip against the bar, elbow bent as he lifted a glass of orange juice to his mouth.

Toni took a step backwards as if to regain her equilibrium. Her breathing immediately felt tight and her stomach went into freefall as she admitted honestly, that physically Rafe Riccardi pushed every one of her buttons.

Steadying herself with a long breath, she went forward. 'Hi...'

Rafe spun round. 'Antonia—' In an almost jerky motion he lowered his arm and placed his glass on the bar top.

For a few seconds there was an awkward silence while they each took stock.

Sweet God, she was lovely, Rafe thought. Beautiful and warm and...sexy. And he wanted her, as he hadn't wanted a woman in ages. Maybe years.

He certainly scrubbed up well. Toni bit gently on the soft pad of her bottom lip. Her eyes flicked to the pale blue shirt that moulded his broad shoulders, followed the tailored line of his black trousers to his black leather shoes. She pressed her clutch-bag tightly against her chest.

'You managed to drag yourself here, then?' Oh, lord. Toni almost groaned. That hadn't come out right. But suddenly her tongue seemed to have a mind of its own.

Rafe gave a tight shrug. 'Bernie Maguire put the weights on me to draw one of the raffle prizes.'

'And you can't very well ignore the chairman of the board,' Toni agreed, oddly disappointed he hadn't felt the need to respond to *her* invitation. 'Our people are mostly at the table over here.' She indicated with her hand. 'Would you like to join us?'

'Thanks.' He picked up his glass. 'Can I get you something to drink while we're here?'

'I'm fine, thanks.' Toni shook her head. 'Have you eaten?'

'I had a steak at the pub.'

Toni flicked a tentative smile at him. 'There's dessert still going begging. Interested?'

'Might be. What's on offer?'

Well, not me. Toni's heart began to patter. Were they

playing games again? 'There are three kinds of bread-and-butter pudding, for starters.'

His chuckle was a bit rusty. 'My grandmother used to make bread-and-butter pudding.'

'Not like this, she didn't.'

'Reckon?' Rafe turned his head a fraction and sent her a slow, lazy smile.

Toni blinked, feeling shock waves of its aftermath right down to her toes. His smile was like the sun coming out. Shame he didn't do it more often. They stopped at the table. 'I'm sitting here.' She put her clutch-bag down. 'Park your drink and let's find out, shall we?'

Rafe hesitated. 'I'm not taking someone's place, am I?'

'I'm not here with anyone.' Toni answered the question she assumed he was asking.

His mouth twitched. 'Lead on, then. I need to see these puddings.'

At the buffet they bypassed a luscious tropical fruit salad, sorbet and various kinds of cheesecakes. 'Now, here we have the bread and butter puddings,' Toni said, hamming it up with a graceful sweep of her hand. 'You could start with maple syrup and pecan, get a bit edgy and try the lemon curd and coconut and then give your tastebuds a real treat and finish with white chocolate and raspberry.'

Rafe clicked his tongue and sighed in mock-resignation. 'It's a hard call but someone has to do it. Going to join me?'

'Of course.' Toni's mouth fell into a soft pout. 'Can't have you eating alone.' With their selections made, they went back to the table.

'So, where are you staying?' Toni asked conversationally.

'Joe and Cath kindly offered me the use of their annexe at the house.'

'What a good arrangement. It's a great space. They

had it built for Joe's dad originally but he didn't stay long. Missed his mates in Sydney.'

'It's certainly very comfortable,' Rafe agreed. 'Close to the hospital. And the pool is a real bonus on these hot nights.'

'Yes, it would be,' Toni rejoined softly, her thoughts going into overdrive. She'd been invited to swim many times in the Lyons' pool. And at night especially it was magical, with the lights by the pool shining back through the tropical shrubbery and edging the white jasmine with soft radiance. And the air you breathed was heavy with woodsy scents. Cath and Joe had created a very private place. Special. She wondered if Rafe found it so.

The creamy dessert slid over her tongue.

Did he swim naked…?

As if he'd divined the pattern of her thoughts, he remarked, 'Joe said you swim at their place quite often. Don't feel you have to stop just because they're away.'

'I wouldn't want to invade your privacy.'

'You wouldn't be. Besides…'His spoon paused midway from his dessert bowl '…it's no fun swimming alone.'

Toni had no time to answer. Bernie Maguire materialised at the table. 'Good, you're both here,' he said. 'We'd like to get cracking if you don't mind and draw these raffles. The mayor will be drawing the main prize and, Rafe, if you'd draw the winners for the cases of wine? And Toni…' He looked down and gave her one of his big barracuda grins. 'Might be a nice touch if you could draw out the winner for the luxury weekend.'

'Me?' Toni's eyes went wide in alarm. 'Bernie, I don't think I should do it. There are more senior people at the hospital—'

'Nonsense.' Bernie clearly wasn't having that. 'It will be very appropriate having a good-looking couple from the hospital on stage. Very appropriate. Right, then.' He rubbed his hands together, indicating mission accomplished. 'I'll just go and get things rolling.'

'This is awful!' Toni glanced despairingly at Rafe. 'We...can't have people thinking we're a couple.'

Rafe shrugged. He could think of worse things. 'Don't worry about it. It's small-town politics. And folk will have found something more interesting to talk about tomorrow.'

Toni had her doubts about that but with Bernie's voice already booming from the stage, inviting everyone to return to their tables for the drawing of the raffle prizes, she got slowly to her feet. The sooner they got this over the better.

With the prizewinners announced, Rafe and Toni squeezed their way through the dancers already back on the floor. They joined Matt and Liz, who were already seated at the table. 'We're just taking a little breather,' Liz said, before introducing Rafe to her husband. She looked in sorrow at her pile of ticket stubs. 'You know, I really thought I was in with a chance to win that luxury weekend.'

'Sorry,' Toni said with dry irony. 'I couldn't seem to find your ticket when I stuck my hand in the barrel.'

The men laughed. 'I'll get another round of drinks in.' Matt got to his feet.

'I'll come with you,' Rafe said. 'But I'll stick to OJ. Antonia?'

'Oh...' Toni felt her cheeks warm. 'Mineral water, thanks.'

As the men walked companionably towards the bar, Liz turned to Toni, her raised brows speaking volumes. 'Antonia?'

Toni rolled her eyes.

Liz smirked. 'Scrubs up well, doesn't he?'

'Matt?' Toni responded innocently.'

'Oh, ha.' Liz made a small face. 'Riccardi, of course. And his voice—smooth as molasses. Do you think—you know?'She rocked her hand expressively. 'He might fancy you?'

Toni felt the nerves in her stomach clench. If the micro-currents already running between them were to be acknowledged, then perhaps she and Rafe Riccardi might just fancy each other. But she wasn't letting Liz get a whiff of that. No way. 'Get over yourself, Lizzy.'

'You looked pretty cosy together up on the stage.' Liz persisted with her banter.

'That was none of my doing. Bernie Maguire insisted. Anyway, enough of this crazy supposition,' Toni said. 'Here come the men with the drinks.'

The conversation between the two couples became general and light and then Matt asked, 'So, Rafe, where were you working before coming here to Forrestdale?' Always the journalist, he'd had begun to sniff out a story.

Rafe looked away, dropping his gaze to his glass, giving the orange juice his riveting attention. 'I've been overseas for the past year, working for Médecins Sans Frontières in Cambodia.'

Liz's arch look at Toni silently said, *So now we know.*

'I imagine the population are still suffering the effects from the reign of that dictator?' Matt considered himself well versed in world politics. 'How is it now?'

Rafe frowned. 'It's still one of the most heavily landmined countries in the world. One in every two hundred and fifty Cambodians has one or more amputations. But for all its tragic history, it's still a beautiful country.'

'Got to have had repercussions for the kids, though?' Matt pressed for more.

'They've lost a whole generation of their skills and professions. Of course it's effected the kids,' Rafe said tersely. 'As we speak, half the country's children are malnourished and one in seven will die before their fifth birthday, mostly from vaccine-preventable diseases.'

Toni felt her breathing falter. Rafe was clearly unsettled. The experience had obviously disturbed him deeply. And as a doctor it would be much worse dealing with so much heartache day after day. She hoped Matt would leave it alone now but of course he didn't.

'What about the basic necessities?' he asked. 'Drinking water? Sanitation?'

'Use your imagination,' Rafe growled.

'I produce a programme on local radio called *Conversations.*' Matt leaned forward eagerly. 'Your experiences working for MSF would make interesting listening. Would you feel like coming over to the studio some time and having a chat with our presenter?'

Rafe's mouth drew in. Probably not. Definitely not. But it wouldn't kill him to be diplomatic. Like him, Matt had a job to do. 'I'll think about it. There's no rush, is there?'

'Take your time.' Matt's shrug was open-handed. 'If, after a chat with Gillian, you don't feel comfortable with the concept, no worries.'

Toni saw Rafe relax—not much, just a slight shift of the muscles under his shirt, but enough to know he was back in control of his emotions. She watched as he drained his drink and rose to his feet.

'I'm going to split, guys. Enjoy the rest of the night.'

Toni's worried eyes followed his exit.

'So, now we know where's he's been.' This time Liz gave voice to her thoughts. 'I wonder if he intends going back?'

'Probably.' Matt's lips twisted into a thoughtful moue.

'Those guys in the front line tend to get addicted to the *cause*.' He bracketed the word in the air.

Toni bristled silently. Quite out of the blue she felt protective of Rafe's privacy. None of them here knew anything about his reasons for going to work for MSF. And she thought that Matt, whatever his best intentions, had ambushed him.

Suddenly, for reasons she couldn't explain, she felt out of sync with her friends. She dredged up an off-key smile and got to her feet. 'All that hard work drawing the raffle prizes has done me, guys. I think I'll call it a night as well.'

'I'll walk you out,' Matt said.'

'No need.' Toni waved away his offer. 'I'm parked close to the front entrance. See you tomorrow, Lizzy. And, Matt, thanks as always for the free publicity for our fundraiser.'

'Hey, any time.' Matt nodded his acknowledgment. 'I'll be sure to pass it along to our station manager. Drive safely.'

Toni fluttered a wave. ''Night.'

Toni's thoughts were unresolved as she drove home. She got that Matt was a facilitator for his programme. And that was fair enough but surely he could have laid off grilling Rafe the way he had?

Damn! Just when Rafe had seemed relaxed enough to start enjoying the evening too. And now he'd probably crawl back into shell and she'd have to start all over again to try to winkle him out so at least they could have some kind of decent working relationship.

She pulled into her carport, killed the engine and went inside. Tossing her clutch-bag on the hall table and kicking off her sandals, she went through to the kitchen. She was wound up. She crossed to the counter and looked through the window at the courtyard. The solar lights had come on, sending the baskets of ferns into feathery silhouettes.

The silvery light reminded her of the Lyons' pool at night. And reminded her that's what she needed right now—to dive into its cool depths and thresh the water until she'd driven off this foul mood of frustration. But she couldn't do that.

Rafe was in residence there.

Rafe heaved himself out of the pool. Standing naked in the moonlight, he shook the moisture from his hair and then bent and picked up his towel from the sun-lounger. Giving his body a cursory wipe, he slung the towel around his hips. He felt better now, his mind freed up from all those images that Matt's questions had dumped all over him.

Padding back along the path to the annexe, he pushed open the screen door and went inside. The place was air-conditioned but so far Rafe had refrained from switching it on. He preferred the weather as it came. And in February it was stinking hot, the air almost brittle with stillness, the pungent smell of ripening mangoes everywhere. So intrinsic of everything Australian, he couldn't get enough of it.

For now, anyway.

CHAPTER FOUR

Next morning.

IN THE clear light of day, Toni decided to put her concerns about Rafe Riccardi into perspective. But concern for his welfare still remained. Perhaps it all boiled down to being a nurse, she decided ruefully. You just couldn't help looking out for others—even adult males.

She took handover and wondered where on earth the rest of her team had suddenly disappeared to.

'Excuse me, Toni?' Samantha stopped at the nurses' station. 'That old guy is back again. What should I do with him?'

Toni looked up. 'You mean Denis?'

Sam nodded. 'The nurses said he only comes in for a chat so should I shoo him off?'

'No, don't do that.' Toni swung off the high swivel stool. 'The one time you do that could be the time he's actually ill. Anyway, we always get him a cup of tea, don't we?'

'I think so.' Samantha looked uncertain. 'I'll do that, shall I?'

'No, we'll have a chat to him first.' Toni glanced at the clock. 'Have you seen the rest of the team, Sam?'

'Uh...' The youngster bit her lip. 'Still in the staffroom, I think.'

'Still?' Toni's brows shot up. It was shaping up to be one of those days and she really didn't need it. She hated having to pull colleagues into line, especially when they'd all turned out last night to support the fundraiser. But rules were there for a purpose and they should know they couldn't come drifting in for their shift whenever they pleased.

Resolutely, she began to walk towards the casualty area where Denis O'Rourke was the only occupant among the rows of padded green chairs.

'Good morning, Denis.' Toni dropped into a chair beside the elderly man. 'How can we help you?'

Denis wheezed a bit. 'Wouldn't mind a cuppa, lovey.'

'Well, that can be arranged.' Toni smiled, lifting his wrist to check his pulse. A bit thready, she decided, and his skin felt hot. She made a tiny moue of concern. 'Are you not feeling well, Denis?'

'Feelin' a bit weak, like. Chest hurts when I breathe...' He tapered off and coughed into a hanky.

'Right.' Toni made a snap decision. 'Let's get a doctor to look at you, shall we? Samantha, here, will take you along to the examination room.'

Where was a doctor when you needed one? Toni cast a slightly exasperated look over the empty unit. Grace Tennant wasn't on duty until later but Justin should have shown his face by now.

'Can I help?'

Toni spun round. The tone of Rafe's voice clearly indicated he'd picked up on her frustration.

To cover her confusion, Toni bit out irritably, 'This place is a shambles this morning. You're in early,' she tacked on almost accusingly. 'Couldn't you sleep?'

'I slept,' he said calmly. And better than he had for a long time. Maybe his demons were beginning to leave him at last. God, he hoped so. He narrowed a look at Toni. 'You obviously didn't.'

She lifted a shoulder. 'Not much.' She'd spent half the night worrying about *him*. Which, looking at him, had been pathetic. Dressed in casual cargo pants and a cotton shirt left open at the neck, he looked upbeat and fresh. Whereas she felt far removed from her usual cheerful persona. 'It was hot,' she affirmed as her reason.

'It was,' he agreed. 'I had a swim before I turned in. You should have come round and joined me.'

And wouldn't that have been just dandy. Her chin snapped up. 'Could you see a patient, please? Justin doesn't seem to be anywhere in sight.'

'Sure. Fill me in.'

'Denis O'Rourke, seventies, regular in Casualty, wanders in for a chat, the odd ailment. We usually give him a bit of attention, a hot drink and send him off.'

Rafe listened attentively. 'So, what's different about your Denis O'Rourke today?'

Toni rolled her bottom lip between her teeth. 'I think he may be brewing something. But, then, maybe I'm wasting your time...'

'You're not wasting my time, Antonia. Trust your instincts. I know I do.'

Their eyes met for an intense moment before each looked away. Awareness, like an imminent thunderstorm, rocked the air between them. Toni breathed in and breathed out and they made their way to the cubicles together.

Rafe was thorough. And Toni felt a rush of gratitude that he'd taken her concern for this lonely old man on board.

Slowly and carefully, Rafe began palpating his patient's stomach. 'That seems fine.' He repositioned the elderly man's worn flannelette shirt. 'Let's have a listen, now.'

Toni gently brought Denis to a sitting position and handed Rafe a stethoscope.

'Thanks,' he murmured. 'Denis, could you manage a cough for me, please? And again. You've a few rattles in there, mate.' Rafe hooked the stethoscope around his neck. 'How long have you been feeling ill?'

'Coupla days…' Denis wheezed. 'Felt real crook when I woke this morning.'

Rafe nodded. 'It's good you came in to see us, then. We'll arrange some treatment for you. Get you feeling fit again.' He went across to the basin to wash his hands, drying them quickly. 'I'd like a word, please, Antonia.'

They stepped outside the cubicle and Toni pulled the curtains closed. She looked questioningly at Rafe.

'Denis is exhibiting early signs of pneumonia,' the registrar said briskly. 'And he's quite seriously dehydrated.'

'So you'll admit him?'

'I'd like to. What's our bed situation?'

'Several for allocation. I've just checked.'

'Excellent.' Rafe pulled out his pen and took the chart Toni handed to him. 'I'd like Denis X-rayed for starters, both bases of lungs. And a sample of sputum, please. We'll see what that tells us.'

'I'll see to it all personally.' It was probably the only way she was going to get anything done today, Toni reflected, a bit tight-lipped.

'The sputum culture may take a while,' Rafe considered, 'so in the meantime we'll start Denis on a drugs regime. We may need to change it slightly when the lab results come back.'

Concern was etched on Toni's face. 'Denis is a great old chap, World War Two veteran. Bit of a loner. He will be all right, won't he, Rafe?'

'Let's hope so.' He began making a notation of the drugs

he wanted used. 'We'll start with Amoxil four-hourly and bensyl six-hourly, both delivered IV.' Clicking his pen shut, he slid it back into his shirt pocket. 'Normal saline to get his fluids back up as a priority. What are his living arrangements like? Do you know?'

'I do, as a matter of fact,' Toni said. 'He was struggling home with his bit of shopping one day and I gave him a lift. He lives in a boarding house. Pretty basic accommodation. Breakfast is a bit of a scratch meal and the rest the residents have to make for themselves.'

'So his nutrition is probably way under what it should be.' Rafe leaned his back against the wall and folded his arms. 'Surely, the Veteran Affairs Department should be looking after his welfare?'

Toni shrugged. 'I doubt if he's ever contacted them. Anything to do with governments takes for ever anyway. He probably preferred to battle on himself.'

'Forrestdale has an excellent aged-care home, doesn't it? Couldn't a placement be found for him there?'

Toni huffed under her breath. 'Someone has to die before a vacancy becomes available there. The place needs extensions urgently. But it all takes money.'

'OK...' Rafe ran a hand across his cheekbones. 'Thanks for the heads up. I'll have a word with Bernie Maguire. He's a big wheel in the Rotary. He may be able to get some action happening. And after he dumped on us last night, he owes us—big time.' Rafe's mouth twitched.

'It wasn't that bad, I suppose,' Toni conceded, her smile a bit strained. It was what happened later when Matt had grilled him that had had her off balance. But she couldn't tell him that. She held up the chart. 'I'll get things under way with X-ray.'

'Thanks. And then perhaps come in for some of my coffee?'

'Sorry, can't.'

Rafe gaze became shuttered. 'Fine.'

Oh, lord—Toni almost ground her teeth. She hadn't meant to sound dismissive but she had more urgent priorities than sitting around, sipping coffee. 'I really have to chase up my nurses and get this place running like a casualty department,' she explained, turning as the electronic doors opened and several walking wounded shuffled in.

Rafe followed her gaze and gave a tight little nod. 'I'll find Justin and tell him to get his butt out here.'

'Thanks.' Toni gave a quick smile but it died on her face. Rafe had already turned and begun walking away.

Toni watched his long-limbed stride down the corridor. Had her acceptance of an invitation to coffee meant that much to him? A mountain of uncertainty engulfed her. She sucked in a deep breath and shook her head. Don't start feeling guilty about this, Toni.

Just don't.

With years of practice, she switched into professional mode, assembling her team and allotting jobs. 'Has anyone seen Liz?' she asked as they began to disperse.

Apparently no one had.

Perhaps she'd gone straight to the station, Toni thought, making her own way there just as Liz sidled in from the opposite end. It was obvious she'd just arrived.

Toni clicked her tongue. 'What time do you call this, Sister Carey?'

'Sorry, I'm late.' Liz shoved her bag under the counter. 'Where do you need me?'

'Where do you want to be?' Toni quipped lightly.

'Dead…' Liz dropped her head into her hands. 'Oh, God, Toni…'

'Oh, my stars!' Toni's voice rippled with speculation. 'Are you hungover?'

'Bit—'

'A bit! Lizzy, you're green!'

Liz groaned. 'My head is spinning.'

'No wonder, you crazy woman.' Toni shook her head in disbelief.

'Don't remind me. But we hadn't been out for ages and the wine was chilled and so lovely…'

'So lovely you now have a king-sized hangover. How's Matt?'

'Creeping round like a wounded crow. Said he's been poisoned.'

Toni got a vivid mental picture and chuckled. 'I can't believe the pair of you! You're not safe out alone.'

Liz held a hand to her tummy. 'Isn't that the truth.'

'Have you taken anything?' Toni became professional.

Liz shook her head.

'Then dose yourself with some paracetamol and go and lie down. I'll call you if I need you.'

'Oh, thank you,' Liz said feelingly. 'I'll make up the time.'

'Don't be ridiculous. Oh, and, Lizzy?'

Liz turned, her eyes large in her pale face. 'Mmm?'

Toni grinned. 'Big drinks of water, OK?'

Liz fled.

Instinct told Toni it was shaping up to be a busy day. She'd just got back to the station after doing a quick tour of cubicles and checking their supplies of IV fluids were adequate when the emergency phone rang.

As she scribbled details, she was conscious of Rafe coming into the nurses' station. He leaned on the counter and waited.

'Workplace accident.' Toni replaced the phone. 'New-build about ten Ks out of town. Patient is a twenty-two-year-old male, Rhys Holland.'

Rafe's mouth tightened. 'What's the injury?'

'Nailgun misfired,' Toni said briskly. 'The nail has apparently gone right through his work boot into the top of his foot.'

Rafe made a dismissive growl in his throat. 'What's the problem with these guys and work tools—are they a bunch of cowboys?'

Toni's mouth drew in. She guessed he was thinking of the fatal workplace accident last week but she didn't appreciate his suggestion that the workers of their country town were less than efficient. 'Ambulance has gone out. They'll have to load the patient so ETA is about thirty minutes.'

'Right. For starters, could you tee up someone from the fire service to come in? We'll need that boot cut off. And I want someone who knows what they're doing.'

Toni bristled. As opposed to a *cowboy* apparently. 'I'll do my best,' she said shortly. 'But it's a voluntary service. It may take a while to locate someone *suitable*,' she emphasised.

'OK.' He gave a cool imitation of a smile, indicating he'd got her point. 'And alert Theatre, please? It sounds like a patch-up job for Keith Sutherland,' he added, referring to the hospital's general surgeon.'

And they'd need a blood specimen and cross-match immediately on arrival, Toni noted silently. Lord, she could do this in her sleep. She began dialling. At last she had joy and Dan Sessarago from the fire service was on his way.

Quickly, Toni assigned Amy to the nurses' station and then drew Harmony aside and filled her in about the incoming emergency. 'Would you like to be involved?' she asked, giving the young grad the option.

'I guess it's the only way I'm going to learn, isn't it?' Harmony looked less than enthusiastic.

'And gain confidence,' Toni agreed.

The nurses hurried towards the ambulance bay. Rafe was already waiting.

'Morning folks.' Erin Pascoe, one of the senior paramedics, sprang lightly from the rear of the vehicle.

Rafe's eyes narrowed. 'Any problems on the way in, Erin?'

'Nothing we couldn't handle. Rhys is not feeling too well, though. We've given Maxolon ten milligrams.'

Toni's gaze flew professionally over the young man. Rhys looked pale beneath his tan. His eyes were closed, clammy perspiration beading his forehead, each breath ending on a little moan.

'Let's move it, please.' Rafe's voice was clipped.

'Cube one is ready.' Toni's response was crisply calm and suddenly, professionally, they were working as a well-oiled team.

'On my count, then, guys.' Erin directed Rhys's transfer to the treatment couch.

'Right, let's get BP and temperature readings, please,' Rafe ordered.

'BP eighty-five on fifty,' Toni reported. 'Temperature thirty-five point five.'

'Thanks. Rhys, can you hear me?'

The young man's eyes fluttered open and closed. He licked his lips. 'Yeah…'

'Any tingling in your arms or legs?'

Rhys shook his head. 'Am I wrecked, Doc?'

'Of course you're not wrecked,' Rafe said bluntly. 'This is a hospital, sunshine. We're here to fix you up.' He turned to Toni. 'Let's get some fluids running, please.'

Toni quickly organised a cannula to run the saline drip. 'What drugs do you need?'

'Make it fifty of pethidine,' Rafe's mouth tightened. 'He's in a bit of pain here.'

Toni handed the keys of the drugs cabinet to Harmony. 'Take Mel with you to double-check. And quick as you can, please.'

'Dan Sessarago.' The fire officer poked his head into the treatment room. 'Let me know when you need me, Doc.'

Rafe's head came up. 'We'll need to stabilise the patient first, mate. Just hang on a tick, would you?'

A few minutes later the medication and saline drip were beginning to do their job. Toni breathed a sigh of relief. 'His colour's improving.' She gave Rafe a guarded smile.

'Mmm.' He seemed distracted. 'Time to get that boot off, I think.'

The fire officer performed the task with speedy expertise. Producing a sharp, thin blade, he sliced through the elastic-sided boot and peeled back the heel. Two forward cuts opened up the front section of the boot. 'If you could steady his leg here, Doc?'

Rafe obliged and all eyes watched as Dan finally eased the flapping pieces of leather away from Rhys's rapidly swelling foot.

'Well done, Dan. Thanks.' Rafe looked searchingly at the damaged foot after Toni had cut through their patient's thick socks with her scissors.

There was soft-tissue damage and an obvious bone fracture. 'What do you think, Harmony?'

'Oh!' Harmony's hand went to her throat. 'It looks very painful. I think I'd have passed out if it had happened to me.'

'Quite possibly.' Rafe's mouth twitched slightly. 'Now, do you think you could organise someone to get a portable X-ray unit down here, please? I don't want Rhys moved unnecessarily just yet.'

'Yes, Doctor.' Harmony flew.

'Thanks for including her.' Toni began gathering up

the bits and pieces from the emergency and swept them into a bin.

Rafe lifted a shoulder as if shrugging off her thanks. 'As you've pointed out to me, Antonia, we're supposed to be a team, aren't we?'

A beat of silence.

Rafe saw her mouth tighten and heard the little staccato hiss of her breath and thought, *Now what?*

'I'll assign another nurse to prepare Rhys for Theatre,' Toni said briefly. 'I need to be elsewhere.'

Toni's expression was tightly controlled as she made her way back to the station. She hadn't appreciated Riccardi's retaliatory *dig* about them being a team. Let's face it, she acknowledged silently, the man just makes me feel unsettled. I need to get my head on straight. Oh, boy, do I ever. And if keeping out of his way for the moment is what it takes, then I'll do it.

'Toni?' Liz caught up with her.

'Feeling better?' Toni came to a halt.

Liz nodded. 'Sorry about all that. It won't happen again.'

'Don't beat yourself up, Lizzy'

'Thanks.' Liz looked relieved. 'Now, where do you need me?'

'There's an emergency in cube one.' Toni went on to give details. 'Riccardi wants the patient's foot X-rayed before they move him, so as soon as that's done, could you help Harmony with Rhys's theatre prep, please?'

'Fine, no worries.'

Liz's antennae began twitching. Why suddenly had *Rafe* become *Riccardi*? Had Toni had a run-in with him? Her friend looked a bit light-lipped. Not like herself at all.

She touched a light hand to Toni's shoulder. 'Hey, why don't you take a break and grab a coffee?'

'Mmm, maybe I will.'

Liz grinned. 'Ed's brought in sticky buns.'

Rafe slammed his car into gear and took off after work, just screeching to a stop in time to allow several people to walk over the zebra crossing. Hell's bells, where was his concentration?

Once home, he stripped off and swam length after length of the pool but that didn't assuage his disquiet. Consequently, he took his unsettled mood to bed with him and lay for ages, staring at the ceiling. But all he saw was Antonia's face. She was offside with him. And he didn't know why. He thumped the pillow in frustration. It was two steps forward and seven back with her, he thought darkly. And he hated it.

He had to clear the air with her. He didn't know how but he would. If not tomorrow, then the next day. But it was almost at the end of her shift on Friday when he got the chance.

Toni had had no difficulty in avoiding Rafe for the rest of the week. She'd had a couple of management meetings elsewhere in the hospital that she'd had to attend and Liz, wanting to make up for her lapse, had offered to be here, there and everywhere. Toni had been more than happy to let her. It did help, of course, that Toni had swapped shifts with a colleague on Wednesday and worked a late shift.

It was now Friday afternoon and she was about to breathe a sigh of relief. She was so looking forward to her weekend. She'd chill out and relax.

And work out what to do about Rafe Riccardi.

A young woman carrying a toddler came into the casualty area almost at the end of her shift and Toni went across to her.

'Hi.' She sent out one of her smiles. 'I'm Toni, one of the nurses. How can we help you?'

'C-could I see a doctor?'

'Of course. I'll just need to get some details. Take a seat and I'll be right back.'

The woman gave her name as Joanne Carter. 'I need to ask about Zoe. She's vomiting everything...' Almost on cue, as though to hurry things along, Zoe began to whimper and pull her little legs up as if in pain.

'Oh, poor sweetheart.' Toni smoothed a twist of fair hair from the little one's forehead. 'Come with me, Joanne.' Toni got to her feet. 'Let's get Zoe more comfortable, shall we?'

Having settled mother and child in one of the treatment rooms, Toni went in search of a doctor. With a bit of luck Grace would be available. But Grace, it seemed, had taken an early mark and gone home.

'Rafe's still around,' Liz said helpfully. 'Want me to bleep him?'

'If you would, please, Lizzy.' Toni took a deep breath. 'Treatment one.'

Oh, lord. There was to be no escape. Her hand went to her heart, finding it over-beating like a trapped bird's. Having to confront Rafe shouldn't be having this effect on her. But there was no getting away from it. It was. She went back to the treatment room. 'Dr Riccardi is on his way, Joanne.'

Rafe strode in, sending a cursory nod to Toni.

'This is Joanne Carter, Doctor.' Toni drummed up a professional face. 'She's concerned about Zoe's vomiting.'

Rafe examined the child carefully. 'What have you been giving Zoe, Mrs Carter?'

'Not much—because she wouldn't take much. I tried

her with her usual milk and a bit of custard—she usually loves that.'

'I'm guessing she threw it right back at you?'

The young mum looked baffled. 'Have I done something I shouldn't? This has never happened before. Zoe is so well usually but now...'

'Do you have a GP?' Rafe asked, thinking he might have been able to get an overview of the family's health.

Joanne shook her head. 'We've only just moved here. My husband was retrenched from his job in Sydney. The job search people sent us here so Brent could get work at the mine. He drives a truck.'

'And where are you living, Joanne?' Rafe gently straightened Zoe's little dress after listening to her tummy.

Joanne looked unhappy. 'At the caravan park. The facilities are pretty basic and the manager is the pits.'

Well, there wasn't much he could do about that, Rafe decided. As soon as the family's finances picked up, they could probably move to somewhere more suitable. Meanwhile, they had to get this little one treated. He took the chart from Toni's outstretched hand and backed up against the couch. 'For the present, I'd like you to keep Zoe off milk and milk products, Joanne. Instead, give her frequent amounts of clear fluids only.'

The young mum nodded. 'How small and how frequent?'

'Good questions.' Rafe's mouth turned up in a fleeting smile. 'Small amounts mean about twenty mils. Do you have a measure at home?'

'I'm not sure.' Joanne bit her lip. 'It's probably in one of the boxes but I haven't found it yet...'

'Not to worry. I'm sure we could spare one from the dispensary.' He shot a questioning glance at Toni.

She nodded, even forcing out a brief smile. 'Not a problem.

'Now, clear means not milk and not solids,' Rafe emphasised. 'Just fluid. I'll give you a note for the chemist. They'll have various mixtures you can add to water. They're especially formulated to replace all the water and chemicals Zoe may lose because of her continual vomiting.'

'I understand,' Joanne said quietly. 'What if she vomits it back, though?'

'OK, if that happens, try diluted lemonade. Say one part to four parts water. If you like, freeze it and make little ice cubes for her to suck. If Zoe can tolerate that, you should see a marked improvement quite soon.'

Joanne looked as though a huge weight had been taken from her shoulders. 'So—how often should I give her the replacement fluids?'

Rafe considered. 'Let's go with every fifteen minutes to start with and then you can lengthen it to thirty minutes if she's keeping it down. If Zoe keeps vomiting, she'll begin dehydrating. In that case, bring her back here to Casualty immediately, day or night, and we'll treat her. All clear?' Rafe sent a rather winning smile at the young mother.

'Yes.' Joanne hesitated and then smiled back. 'Thank you so much, Doctor.' Getting to her feet, she scooped Zoe out of Toni's arms. 'I'll get this started straight away.'

'Good.' Rafe went ahead and pulled back the curtains. He hesitated, momentarily disturbed by a sudden train of thought, and turned back. 'Use bottled water for the time being, Joanne.'

'Oh—' Joanne bit the underside of her lip, looking disconcerted. 'I'll—um—get some on the way home.'

Toni ushered the young mother out. 'Take a seat back

in the waiting area, Joanne. I'll just grab that measuring glass for you.'

Toni took off at speed and Rafe had to call her twice before she registered he was following her. She stopped and waited, only turning when he came abreast. 'Did you want something else?'

'I did.' Rafe planted his hands firmly on his hips. 'I'm about to email an urgent directive to all shifts of A and E. Would you see it's printed out and displayed where it'll be seen?'

Toni gave a twisted smile. 'And hopefully *read*?'

'Mmm, that too,' he agreed dryly.

Toni frowned a bit. 'I heard what you said to Joanne about using bottled water. Do you think we're in for more cases of gastro?'

'Seeing that little kid so ill set off a few alarm bells.' His thoughts turned dark for a second. 'Where I was stationed in Cambodia, gastro was a constant source of concern but with our standard of living it's not so prevalent. All the more reason when we come across a case, to exercise vigilance, especially amongst the very young and the aged.'

'But surely if it's something to do with the water, we'd all be sick,' she suggested.

Rafe wasn't prepared to go any further with supposition. 'Just let's get the staff alerted to the possibility, and if any more cases present over the weekend, we'll take it from there and start investigating.'

Toni nodded. 'I'll let you get on, then.'

'Antonia...' Suddenly, Rafe felt every nerve in his body jerk to attention, his heart jostling for space inside his chest. But he had to do this now. 'Could we talk—properly?'

Toni stiffened and went very still, almost *feeling* the

silence hanging between them like an unexploded bomb. She moistened her lips. 'Where?'

Spurred on by her acceptance, Rafe tried to think on his feet. 'Not here.'

'No.'

Well, at least they'd agreed on that. 'We're both off shift shortly. Come round for a swim.'

A beat of silence.

'Don't think so.' Toni heard her voice oddly calm and decisive.

'OK…' Rafe rubbed a hand across his forehead. Obviously too far, too fast. 'Somewhere you'd feel comfortable, then.'

Toni hesitated briefly. 'Perhaps the café in the main street? The Copper Kettle. It's a couple of doors down from the supermarket.'

'Fine.' His green eyes lit briefly. 'See you there in about twenty?'

'Make it twenty-five,' Toni countered. After all, a girl had to make herself presentable.

CHAPTER FIVE

Toni looked at her nurse's uniform of smoky blue shirt and navy trousers and made a face in the mirror, wishing that today of all days she'd brought a change of clothes to work. But she hadn't expected Rafe's invitation. Not for a second.

She'd have to make do with brushing her hair into some kind of order and refreshing her lip gloss.

She couldn't quite believe that in a few minutes she'd be meeting Rafe outside the hospital.

Suddenly her heartbeat reflected her slight panic. But she was glad he'd made the first move. They certainly could not have gone on in the kind of energy-sapping vacuum that had sprung up between them.

Sitting in one of the high-backed booths in the café, Rafe found his gaze hovering impatiently on the entrance. He tried to get a grip on his wayward thoughts. He prided himself on always being focused in the course of his working day but almost from the moment Antonia had turned that amazing smile on him, he'd found his thoughts wandering off at the most unexpected moments. Wild thoughts, he admitted, his gut turning over again. Thoughts of a man and a certain woman…

He sucked in a deep breath and looked around him, for the first time noticing a group of girls sitting across the aisle. They were obviously students. Rafe recognised their blue and white checked uniforms as being from the local high school. They were slurping drinks out of old-fashioned soda glasses, their girlish chatter constant. Perhaps this was their after-school Friday ritual, he thought wryly, reflecting on his own high school years in Sydney. They'd been good years. Happy years.

But then *life* had happened…

A subdued shriek from the girls' booth abruptly refocused his run into the past. Rafe gave them an enquiring under-brow glance. They were all busy with their mobile phones.

'Luke's texted me!'

Obviously the owner of the shriek, Rafe decided, his mouth tilting into something that was almost a smile.

'He wants to go out!'

'Oh, my God!' Another shriek from another of the girls. 'You cow!'

Obviously, a compliment. Rafe felt his mouth twitch again.

'It'll take me, like, *hours* to get ready! And I've a zit on my chin!'

'The chemist's got concealer on special,' someone said helpfully.

'I'm broke until I get my pay tomorrow!' Luke's date, dramatically.

'I can lend you twenty bucks.' The helpful one again.

'Cool! Let's go, then.'

Decision made, they rose as one in a flurry of arms, legs and backpacks. And female solidarity.

God, they learn it from the cradle, Rafe thought broodingly. And then, as he watched the girls' giggly progression towards the exit, he caught sight of Toni at the entrance. Oh, hell. He struggled with an odd sense of unreality. With the afternoon sun streaming behind her and backlighting her, she looked like an angel.

Almost dazedly, he half rose, watching as the girls stood back for Toni to come in. 'Hi, Toni,' they chorused.

'Hi, girls.' Toni smiled, returning their finger waves as she slipped past them. She headed straight along the aisle to Rafe's booth. 'Sorry, I'm a bit later than I thought.'

'It's fine.' Rafe caught the tail end of her smile and they sat down together. 'I didn't mind the wait. I had free entertainment on tap.'

'The girls?' She laughed softly. 'They're gorgeous.'

'You know them?'

'Mmm.' Toni slid into the corner of the booth. 'I do the relationship talk at the high school.' She gave him a wide-eyed look. 'We cover health issues, *et cetera*.'

Rafe merely raised an eyebrow in acknowledgment. Young adults needed to be properly informed and in this day and age any health talk worthy of the name had to cover issues like safe sex. 'I'm sure you do it very well.' *Idiot*. Rafe groaned inwardly at his loaded comment.

'Oh, I do.' She smiled, activating the tiny dimple beside her mouth. She took up the menu. 'Now, what are we having? What about a pot of tea?'

Rafe scrubbed lean fingers across his cheekbones, trying to concentrate. 'Sounds good.'

'And a slice of chocolate cake?'

His lips twitched. 'What with bread and butter pudding the other night and now chocolate cake, I'm beginning to think you have a sweet tooth, Antonia.'

She shrugged. 'I do. But I exercise so it evens out.'

'I guess it does.' Rafe looked up as the waitress appeared at their table. He gave their order and then placed the menu carefully down on the table top. 'Thanks for coming, by the way.'

She raised an expressive eyebrow at him. 'What did you want to talk about?' As if she didn't know.

'I haven't seen you about much this week. Have you been avoiding me?'

Wow, that was direct. Toni felt a slick of embarrassment. 'Being nurse manager, I'm sometimes out of the department. You weren't inconvenienced, were you?'

'Professionally, no.' Rafe gave her a long, intense look. 'Personally…' he lifted a shoulder expressivel. '…I, uh, thought I might have offended you and you were keeping out of my way.'

'I was,' Toni heard herself say, and looking back at her motivations now, it all seemed a bit pathetic. And professionally it had been way out of line. 'My apologies.'

Rafe felt the wind taken right out of his sails. He hadn't expected her to be so upfront. But, then, how well did he know Antonia Morell? Not as well as he wanted to, that was certain. The admission unsettled him. He took a deep swallow. 'Was it something I said to make you upset in the first place?'

Toni expelled a sigh, recognising that this was a time when only the truth would do. 'Things got a bit ratty the day after the Valentine party. I hadn't slept well and my team and your resident were all over the place like recalcitrant children—'

'And I came in all upbeat and cheerful. I remember now. You were snippy.'

'I hadn't slept well,' she reiterated.

'Was there a reason—apart from the hot weather? You weren't drinking, as I recall.'

For heaven's sake! Toni almost rolled her eyes. What was this, an inquisition? She wasn't in the principal's office but it sure felt like it. *I was concerned about you!* She felt like letting him have it straight between the eyes. But that would be admitting she more than liked him. And she wasn't admitting that—not even to herself.

'It was just one of those things,' she said finally. 'I don't do late nights very well.'

She didn't do late nights? What kind of a ridiculous answer was that? Her job consisted of shift work, for God's sake. Rafe was still thinking about a response when their waitress arrived with their tea and cake.

'Oh, good,' Toni sidetracked quickly, thankful for the reprieve from his questions. 'Nice teacups instead of mugs. That's a change.' Taking up the pot, she began to pour. 'How do you take your tea?'

'Just black, thanks.'

'Oh, me too. Do you have the weekend off?'

A fleeting frown touched his eyes. 'Apart from a multi-trauma happening, I believe so.'

'So, any plans?' She passed his tea across the table. 'Are you hoping to see something of the district while you're here?'

'I'd like to.' Rafe was thoughtful. He knew when he'd been snowed. And the lady had done a brilliant job. But he wasn't without ammunition. 'Would you like to be my guide?'

Toni's mouth fell open. That invitation had come out of left field. It would mean spending the whole day with him. Was she up for it? When in doubt, don't. Her mother's invocation came back to her. But what was she, for heaven's sake? A woman or a wimp? He was new in town. It wouldn't hurt her to be friendly. 'OK...' she said slowly. 'This part of the country is steeped in history. There are a few interesting places we could visit. I'll have a bit of a think and have an itinerary planned for tomorrow.'

'Don't go overboard.' He flashed her a mocking kind

of look. 'I'd prefer to keep things slow and easy.' His eyes gleamed with lazy intent.

Toni's heart hitched to a halt. 'I'll...bear that in mind.'

They made desultory conversation over their afternoon tea. Then Toni looked at her watch. 'I'm going to split. I need to do a quick swoop at the supermarket.' She gathered her bag and got to her feet. 'Thanks for the tea.'

'Thanks for the conversation—and the enlightenment.' Their eyes met and he could see the wariness in her gaze. 'See you tomorrow.'

Toni hovered. 'About ten suit you?'

'Ten o'clock is fine. I don't know where you live or I'd offer to pick you up.'

Then it might feel like a real date and Toni wasn't having that. 'Might be quicker and easier if I come round to you,' she said.

'Whatever makes you happy, Antonia,' he said sardonically.

She took a deep breath, about to flutter a little wave but thought better of it. Instead, she gripped the strap of her shoulder bag so hard her fingers almost turned blue. She offered a guarded kind of smile. 'Well—bye, then.'

He merely lifted a finger and nodded.

'Sleep well!'

Toni heard the laughter in his voice as he called after her. Her sense of triumph faltered. He hadn't believed her explanation for her tardiness. Hadn't believed her at all. Well, one to you, Doctor, she apportioned fairly. Grabbing a trolley, she shot into the supermarket and stood gaping. She'd completely forgotten what she'd come to buy.

Toni chose a soft, flirty sundress for her day out. She'd made herself eat museli and fruit for breakfast, despite her stomach leading her on a merry dance of its own. Stepping into flat-heeled sandals, she looked in the mirror, startled to see the slight flush in her cheeks. Well, she could tame that but there was nothing she could do about the light of expectancy in her eyes.

Oh, lord. She'd vowed to be practical and level-headed about this day out with Rafe. Instead, her image reflected a wide-eyed vulnerability. Get a grip, Toni, she warned silently. You've been round this track once before, remember?

But then again, Rafe wasn't a two-timing rat like Alex, was he...?

She turned away, collecting bits and pieces for her hold-all, pausing as her eyes lit on the red and white bikini draped across the back of her bedroom chair. Without thinking twice, she picked up the brief garment and tossed it into her bag.

They might swim and they might not. But she'd be prepared. And the bikini might be brief but not that brief and it was comfortable and allowed her the freedom of feeling part of the water without being naked. Clipping on a big colourful sports watch, she made her way outside to the car port.

It took only a few minutes to get across town to the Lyons' place. Rafe's vehicle, a modest, black SUV, was already outside and waiting. Toni parked neatly behind it, took a few breaths to centre herself and got out of the car.

Weather-wise the morning was perfect, she decided. Sultry but perfect. For a moment she stopped, lifting her head and listening. Already the cicadas were up and about, whirring madly in the shrubbery, the air, when she breathed it in, was summery hot and sharp with the tang of lemon-scented tea trees.

And promise.

* * *

Rafe was waiting for her in the courtyard in front of the annexe. Had been for the past thirty minutes. He was sitting in one of the comfortable outdoor chairs, pretending to read a surfing magazine one of the Lyons kids had left behind.

It was useless. He couldn't concentrate. And his stomach was giving him gyp. He'd forced down a bacon sandwich that now felt like cement in his gut.

He was a lunatic. What had possessed him to think he was ready to start dating again?

But it wasn't really a date.

Yes, it was.

No, it wasn't…

He'd be cool. He'd be cool.

Relax, then.

He leaned back in his chair, one leg jiggling restlessly. He glanced at his watch and swore. Where the hell was she?

She came round the corner, her step silent across the lawn. She saw Rafe waiting. 'Morning,' she called across the short distance that separated them. 'You're ready, I see.'

Rafe jackknifed to his feet as if he'd been stung. 'You're late!' He squirmed inwardly. God, he'd barked at her.

Toni wasn't having that. 'I'm never late. Your watch must be fast.' And this was a ridiculous conversation. Another one. She lifted a hand and placed it against the lattice screen. And looked at him. He was dressed in baggy cargo shorts and a soft, pale blue polo shirt that showed up the deep tan of his arms and throat. She took a shallow breath, all her nerve-ends quivering. Mentally, she drew back, wanting them to get moving, get on their way, but her feet felt anchored. All she could do was to absorb the proud set of his head, the ripeness of his masculine bearing and the way he was looking at her mouth. Automatically, she moistened her lips. 'It's hot out there. You'll need a hat.'

'I have one in the car.' Sweet God. Rafe took a steadying breath. In her pretty dress, with her hair flowing, her glowing skin and that sweet, very sweet mouth, she wouldn't be out of place in a painting. Perhaps in a field, picking daisies. Or frolicking with lambs. Something stirred inside him. Something that hadn't been stirred in a long time. Something that had been breathed into life the moment Antonia Morell had smiled at him.

'Ready, then?' Toni removed the sunglasses from the top of her head and twirled them in her fingers.

'Yep.' Rafe broke out of the fanciful daydream. Touching his back pocket, he located his wallet. 'I'll… just shut the door.' He did, precisely and quickly, and then they were striding across the lawn and back to the path. At least Rafe was striding.

'Where's the fire?' Toni asked dryly.

'Sorry.' Rafe slowed, catching a drift of her flowery shampoo for his trouble. 'Force of habit.'

He released the catch on the double gates that led to the footpath and waited for her to go through then followed her and shut the gates. He turned and stopped abruptly, eying her pewter-coloured sports car. He whistled under his breath. 'You drive a BMW?'

'A birthday present from my parents,' she said airily. 'They've a thing about road safety. I'm presuming you want us to go in your car?'

'I'd prefer to drive, if you wouldn't mind?'

Toni shrugged. 'I'll navigate. Hang on a tick. I'll just get my bag.'

Settling into the passenger seat of his car, Toni adjusted her seat belt and then, looking up, gave him a quick smile. 'How do you want to do this?'

'I'm sure you have a plan, Antonia.'

His reciprocal smile left a lingering warmth in his eyes and Toni felt her heart lurch. 'I thought perhaps we could follow a stretch of the old Cobb and Co. route,' she said, referring to Australia's first method of transportation.

'Back to the horse and coach days,' he reflected. 'Sounds good. Where to first, then?'

'About twenty Ks out to a township called Maeburn. They've re-created one of the coaches and have it on display. There's also a gorgeous church, St Anne's, supposed to be the oldest timber church in the state. Well worth a look, I think.'

Rafe needed no further encouragement. To spend time with her away from the hospital was going to be a heady experience. He couldn't wait.

In the close confines of his car Toni made herself relax. She guessed she was going to get to know a different Rafe Riccardi today. They'd sparred a bit already and she liked that. And he smelled nice, she decided. Soap and water nice. She flicked him a query. 'I'm supposed to be the navigator, so do you want me to keep up a running commentary or…?' She stopped and shrugged.

'Tell me a bit about Cobb and Co.,' he said, his eyes firmly on the road.

Surely, he was kidding. 'Didn't you learn Australian history at school?'

'Not much of it. We concentrated mostly on British history. When I left school, I could recite all the kings and queens of England but I couldn't tell you who our first PM was.'

'That's appalling, Rafe!'

'I agree,' he said with equanimity. 'But things have changed a bit now, I believe.'

'One would hope so.' She huffed a derogatory laugh. 'I'll bet you went to one of those exclusive boys' schools.'

He named it and she huffed again.

'I gather you were much more enlightened, then?' He teased.

'I went to a progressive, co-ed high school where we *did* learn Australian history,' she told him with a little curl of satisfaction.

'So, forgive my ignorance, then.' He laughed. 'And tell me about Cobb and Co.'

Toni was more than happy to launch into her spiel. 'Just stop me if I'm boring you, though,' she warned.

'You could *never* bore me, Antonia,' he said with a certainty that left her head spinning.

'OK…' She took a steadying breath. 'Cobb and Co. began in the 1850s in Victoria. Gold had just been discovered, so their prime purpose was to get folk from Melbourne to the diggings. As well as passengers, they carried the Royal Mail and a bit of freight.'

'And when did they come here to New South Wales?' Rafe wanted to know.

'Around the 1860s, apparently. And then Queensland after that. To travel, say, fifty miles, they had a team of forty horses. They had to change the teams regularly to give the horses a spell.'

Rafe was thoughtful. 'So, allowing for the vastness of our country, the company must have had a huge number of horses to cope with the distances they had to travel.'

'Thousands. And they had their own workshops where they built and maintained their coaches, and had hundreds of drivers and grooms. And you had to book days in advance, of course, to get a seat on the coach.'

'No going online, then.' He laughed. 'How long did the company operate?'

'Seventy-five years, they say. What a unique part of our history, though. Don't you agree?'

'Absolutely. But when you imagine some of those roads back then…'

'Makes you pleased we now have nice comfortable cars with upholstered seats,' she said with a laugh.

'Mmm. Thanks, that was great,' he said. 'Go on with your travelogue.'

'That's enough for now,' she countered. 'Tell me about you.'

'Ah…' Rafe felt his shoulders tense. He wasn't sure he wanted to go there. The whole idea of having this day out had been to get away from *himself.*

'Surely you're not modest, Dr Riccardi?' Toni sent him a teasing look.

No, he wanted to tell her. Just *private.* But obviously that wasn't going to satisfy the lady.

But before he could open his mouth she said chattily, 'Well, judging by the school you went to, you were obviously brought up in Sydney, right?'

'Right.' He forced a smile. 'Dover Heights, to be precise.'

'Oh, *very* nice. My family lives in Rose Bay,' Toni said. 'We must have been practically neighbours. Do you have siblings?'

'One brother, Ben. He's a freelance photo journalist. He travels the world.'

'I guess you'd have to be a certain kind of person to do that for a living,' Toni reflected. 'I'd prefer having roots, I think.'

Rafe kept his own counsel. This was way too deep and meaningful for the present fluid state of his life. 'What about you?' He changed tack skilfully. 'Any siblings?'

'Just me,' she said lightly.

His mouth crimped at the corners. 'Were you indulged?'

'I wouldn't have thought so. Mum and Dad are pretty grounded. Dad's an ENT consultant and Mum is a professional fundraiser for several charities.'

'Must be where you got your organisational ability,' Rafe suggested. 'Did you always want to be a nurse?'

She made a small face. 'I actually did a year and a half of medicine. As students, we were thrown out on to the wards pretty early. And when I saw the hands-on skills of the nurses, I figured that's where I wanted to be. I chucked medicine and enrolled in nursing.'

'Well, you excel at it,' he complimented her.

She blushed. 'Thanks. I like the feeling of being able to get things done for the patients, I suppose. What about you?' She turned a querying look on him. 'Are you from a medical background?'

'No.' He gave an amused chuckle. 'My dad's a bookie.'

'How interesting. What was it like growing up for you?'

He shrugged. 'It was good. Sometimes Ben and I pencilled for Dad at the races. That was an experience.'

'I can imagine…' Toni drifted off.

'My mother is an artist.'

Toni heard the pride in his voice. 'Fantastic. Does she exhibit?'

'She does and she actually has a small gallery in Rose Bay.'

'How incredible! I've probably walked past it a million times.'

'You should have walked *in*,' Rafe countered.

'Next time I'm down, I certainly will. And buy something,' she added on a laugh. Oh, lord, this was surely kismet. She and Rafe must have walked the same streets, swum at the same beaches. She might have passed him in the corridors of a Sydney hospital some time. But no.

She'd have remembered that. Perhaps they had been des-tined to meet. But for what reason? She sobered. Time wasn't on their side. He was on the move. She wanted to put down roots. It was crazy to think they could ever be more than...friends.

Rafe flicked her a discerning look. 'You've gone very quiet, Antonia.'

For answer, she pointed to a sign up ahead. 'That's our turn-off for Maeburn. Just keep following the wagon-wheel logo directional signs. And I don't talk *all* the time,' she countered. 'Anyway, you've gone a bit quiet yourself.'

'Just thinking.'

'Care to tell me?'

Rafe felt his gut tighten. He couldn't possibly tell her that having her sitting next to him like this made his world feel right. And that if he didn't kiss her before the day was out, he'd go crazy. Instead, he managed a laugh of sorts. 'Maybe I'll tell you later.'

Very soon, they entered the township of Maeburn and Toni directed Rafe to a parking area from where they could walk to the various places of heritage interest. Rafe pro-duced bottles of water from a cooler in the boot of the car and they began their tour.

The timber coach was painted a distinctive maroon with gold trim. It stood in a Perspex enclosure in the main street. Rafe and Toni joined the little knot of tourists viewing. 'It's smaller than I imagined,' Rafe said. 'That kind of dicky-seat at the rear was obviously intended for any overflow of passengers or freight.'

Toni pretended to shudder. 'Imagine being caught in a thunderstorm and having to sit out there. Or being preg-nant and having to go over those rough roads.'

'Mmm.' Rafe took a long swallow of his water. 'Our forebears were certainly made of stern stuff.'

Toni looked thoughtful. 'I guess we all try to do our best with the circumstances we're faced with. Or I'd like to think we do.'

He gave a hard-edged laugh. 'That's far too weighty to discuss on such a nice day. Come on, Ms Morell.' He touched a hand to her shoulder. 'What else do you have to show me on this tour?'

'Let's do the church.' Toni could still feel the imprint of his fingers as they moved away. 'We cut through this little park at the end of the street,' she said in her role of official guide.

'And after we've seen the church, we'd better find somewhere to eat lunch.'

Toni sent him a teasing smile. 'I thought you might have packed us a picnic.'

'Not today.' His mouth folded in on a dry smile. 'But don't think I couldn't.'

She gave a throaty laugh. 'I'll hold you to that.'

Oh, I hope you will, Antonia, Rafe told himself fervently. *I hope you will.*

They took the path that ran between two beautiful old ghost gums, crested a gentle rise in the ground and stood looking across at St Anne's. The gracious old timber structure was set prettily among lawns and flower beds.

'Shall we go in?' Toni said.

Rafe hesitated. 'Are you sure it's open?'

'Of course it's open. It's only locked at night. And, amazingly, there's never been any kind of vandalism.'

'So the angels are guarding it, are they?' he responded, tongue in cheek.

Toni rolled her eyes. 'We'll go in through the side entrance.'

Rafe felt an odd kind of peace when they entered the old church. His gaze tracked to the stained-glass windows where the early afternoon sun streamed through, making dappled patterns on the light maple wood of the pews.

'Look up,' Toni whispered. 'The whole ceiling is pressed metal.'

'Impressive.' Rafe took in the dome-shaped ornate ceiling. 'When was the church built, do you know?'

'Nineteen-ten,' Toni replied without hesitation. 'Given its height, erecting that ceiling would have been quite a task for the builders back then. And here at the rear of the church is the choir loft.'

Rafe moved closer, to better appreciate the intricate carving along the rails of the staircase leading up to the choir. 'It's very beautiful,' he murmured.

Toni nodded. 'Would you like to sit for a minute? It's nice to just *be,*' she added softly.

Rafe was like putty in her hands. He followed her into one of the pews and let the peace and tranquillity surround him. It had been a long time since he'd felt so relaxed, he thought, letting the burdens of the past slide away.

Toni was in her own little well of peace. This place never failed to do it for her and she'd been here many times. She glanced at Rafe, her gaze flicking all the way down his body and back again. He turned his head and they shared a smile, tremulous, hardly there. 'Thanks,' he said deeply. Toni gave a quick nod. She knew exactly what he meant.

No more words were needed.

As they left the church, Toni wondered how her hand had crept into his. But it had and he seemed determined to keep it there.

The day was beginning to take on a magic quality of its own, Rafe thought. He took a deep breath and asked lightly, 'Is that a barbecue I can smell?'

'One of the pubs does a special outdoor lunch on

Saturdays,' Toni informed him with a grin. 'I can see you're interested.'

'Certainly. Aren't you?'

'Yes, thank you,' she answered sweetly. 'It's only a short stroll from here to the pub. Lunch is served in a beer garden kind of setting so the surroundings are nice and cool.'

'This is terrific,' Rafe said, as they made their way past a wall of tropical fern into the lattice-enclosed beer garden.

'And there's a free table,' Toni pointed out happily.

Rafe squeezed her hand. 'Grab it and I'll get us a drink. Light beer?' His dark brows rose in quick query.

'Perfect. Thanks.'

A little while later they touched glasses and sampled the icy-cold ale. Then set about collecting their food from the barbecue. Toni wasn't surprised when Rafe selected a prime T-bone steak while she herself preferred the char-grilled chicken. There were several kinds of salads on offer so, selections made and plates loaded, they made their way back to their table.

'Oh, yummy.' Toni made a show of licking her lips in anticipation. 'I'm starving.'

Rafe looked amused. 'Did you skip breakfast?'

'Uh-uh. Never do. Did you?'

He may as well have for all the good it had done. He lifted a shoulder in dismissal.

She tinkled a laugh. 'Were you uptight about coming out with me today?'

Hell. Was she a witch or something? 'I haven't been on anything resembling a date for a long time,' he admitted.

'So, this is a date, then?' Toni brought her head up, her look teasing.

'What else would you call it?' he growled, prodding a chunk of tomato with his fork.

Unabashed, Toni chuckled softly. 'I'd call it a date.'

They went on with their meal, talking inconsequentially, tuning in, tuning out, idle talk, getting-to-know-each-other kind of talk.

Toni didn't realise how engrossed they'd become in their conversation until a sharp, desperate plea broke the air of happy relaxation in the beer garden.

'Could someone help me?' A man thrust forward, curving a path between the tables. 'Is there a doctor here? Or a nurse?'

'I'm a doctor.' Rafe was immediately on his feet. 'What's happened?'

The man took a hard breath to compose himself. 'We were on a hot-air balloon flight—struck turbulence—it's come down in the park. My daughter, Simone—she's hurt—it's bad—'

'Get my bag, Toni!' Rafe fished out his keys from the pocket of his shorts and tossed them across to her. 'It's in the boot. The park? You'll know where to come?'

'I'll know.' Toni ran.

'Geoff Mullins.' The man bit out the introduction as they ran from the beer garden and across the road to the park.

'Rafe Riccardi. How old is your daughter, Geoff?'

'Simone's eighteen today. The balloon ride was a birthday surprise. Wish now we'd never gone on the bloody thing—'

'Did you hit something on the way down?' Rafe was already formulating possible injuries in his mind.

'Tree. Bloody great branch broke off and got Simone under her ribs. Hell, Doc...' The father's voice broke. 'She's my little girl...'

Rafe wasted no time in commiserating. What could he say anyway until he'd seen the girl? Following Geoff's lead, he put on a fresh burst of speed as the crashed balloon came into sight, the basket lurching drunkenly on its side. A cluster of bewildered passengers was hovering nearby.

'Geoff! Oh, thank God!' A woman, obviously the mother, was cradling Simone on the ground. She looked a desperate plea at Rafe. 'Can you help?'

'I'm a doctor.' He dropped down beside the injured girl. One swift, comprehensive glance told him they were in trouble of the worst kind. 'Hi, Simone,' he said gently. 'I'm Rafe.'

'Can't breathe,' she rasped. 'Hurts…sick…'

Rafe jerked up from his kneeling position. 'Has someone called an ambulance?' he yelled to the watching crowd.

A young man raised his hand. 'I called. There's one on the way from Forrestdale. Can I do anything?'

'Just keep a look out, mate, and direct them, if you would?'

'Can do.'

Rafe went back to his patient.

'Everything's blurry…' Screwing her eyes closed, Simone struggled to find air.

'My friend's gone to get my medical case, Simone. I'll be able to help you in a minute. Just hang in there. Good girl.'

'Here's your bag!' One hand on her chest, breathy from her run, Toni's experienced eye took in the emergency at a glance. Heard the girl's laboured breathing. She dropped beside Rafe. 'Pneumothorax?'

'Looks like it.' Rafe shot open his case and drew out his stethoscope. 'Simone, I need to listen to your chest.'

'Unn…' Simone mumbled, struggling harder for breath.

'Please…' The mother whispered. 'What's happening with my daughter?'

'Simone has a punctured lung, Mrs Mullins. That's why

she's having so much trouble breathing. Now, we have an emergency here and we can't wait for the ambulance.'

On a groan of anguish Geoff Mullins took his daughter's hand and pressed it against his cheek. 'What are you gonna do, Doc?'

'I'm going to put a needle in. It'll help Simone to breathe more freely.'

'Oh, God...' The father's distress was painful to see. 'Will it hurt?'

Toni stepped in. 'It'll hurt but only for second.' Already she could see Rafe's fingers working their way down Simone's ribcage. He stopped.

'There?'

He nodded.

Toni swabbed the coolness of alcohol on the girl's skin and watched as the needle pierced her chest and broke through into her lung.

'You're OK, now Simone.' Rafe was taping the needle into place as he spoke. 'Just stay very still for me while I make sure it's secure.'

'Mmm...better,' Simone croaked.

'Don't try to talk,' Toni said gently. 'Once the ambulance gets here, we'll get you on some oxygen. In the meantime, folks, could we get Simone more comfortable?'

The parents, who'd been wearing warm clothing to compensate for the high altitude of the balloon flight, immediately whipped off their coats and helped Toni fold them under the injured girl's head.

'Better...' Simone raised the ghost of a smile. 'Thanks...'

'When you get to the hospital, they'll give you a proper chest tube and and X-ray,' Rafe said gently. 'You've been very brave, kiddo.'

'Thank you so much, both of you.' The mother drew shaky fingers across her eyes.

'Yeah—thanks,' Geoff added gruffly. 'Mighty job.'

Rafe shrugged. 'Just glad we were here. What about you and the rest of the passengers? Are you all right?'

'Bit shocked, I think,' Mrs Mullins said. 'The pilot's gone to call his base. He's upset, poor man.'

'Poor man! I'll sue his butt off,' Geoff growled. 'We could have all been killed.'

'Geoff, let it go,' his wife pleaded. 'It was an accident. The company will be insured. I'm sure we'll get compensation or whatever it is they do.'

'Ambulance is here!' someone shouted.

Rafe turned to Toni. 'I'll go with Simone to the hospital. Could you follow in my car?'

'Sure.' They exchanged a private kind of smile. 'Quite an eventful end to our day out!'

'It's not over yet, Antonia,' he countered, and his voice was soft, muted, almost a seductive caress that wound itself around her like the finest strands of silk as they stood in the sun-filled park on that Saturday afternoon.

CHAPTER SIX

KEITH SUTHERLAND was waiting for them in Resus. Looking at Rafe following along behind the ambulance trolley, he shook his head. 'What is it with you guys? Not content with emergencies coming to you, you go out and find them instead.'

'All the time,' Rafe said dryly. 'Keith, this is Simone Mullins, aged eighteen.' Rafe continued to give a brief handover. 'Her parents will be here directly.' He placed his hand gently on Simone's wrist. 'Dr Sutherland will take care of you now, Simone. I'll look in on you tomorrow to see how you're doing. Meantime, take it easy, all right?'

Simone's eyelids flickered and closed. ''Anks...' was all she could manage.

Toni was waiting in the car park.

Rafe piled into the driver's seat and they took off.

'How is she?' Toni asked.

'Exhausted. But she'll be fine.'

Toni sent him a quick look. 'Where are we going now?'

'Back to my place,' he said shortly. 'Let's try and salvage something from the rest of the day. Fancy a swim when we get there?'

'Yes...' Toni said on a long breath. 'Sounds wonderful.'

'Do you need to call in at home for your swimmers?'

'Not really,' Toni deadpanned. 'I thought we could swim in the nude.'

Rafe's jaw fell open. His heart gave a sideways skip. Was she serious?

'But maybe not.' She laughed softly. 'Had you going there, didn't I?'

He conceded a smile at that. Just a small one. 'Oh, you'll keep,' he said. But rather than a threat, he made it sound like a promise.

'I'm going to relish this swim.' Toni swung her bag, as they made their way along the path to the annexe.

Rafe opened the door and they went in.

'May I use your bedroom? Toni dragged a hand through her hair and eased it away from the back of her neck. 'I'll just slip into my bikini.'

She wore a bikini? Sweet God, what was she trying to do to him? Desire and very basic need slammed into him like a great breath of scorching wind.

'What?' Toni felt her throat dry. He was staring at her mouth as though it was beckoning him, bewitching him. In a nervous reaction she released her fingers, letting her bag fall in a crumpled heap to the floor.

Suddenly *everything* had changed between them.

Toni felt all her senses come to life, flaming into response as Rafe moved closer, moved into her personal space, so close she could feel his breath on her cheek.

The weight of a kiss that simply had to happen was only a whisper away.

Rafe took her face in his hands. He bent to her, his lips teasingly missing hers, moving instead slowly along her cheek, her jaw, her throat, savouring every part of her skin, the weight of his lips so close—daring her to respond.

How could she resist?

Her lips turned to his like petals to the sun and the wild,

beautiful weight of his mouth was on hers. The cool control of his tongue was parting her lips, meeting the tip of hers and slowly coiling, tasting.

Toni sighed, feeling his hand guiding her, nestling in the small of her back. And she didn't let herself think whether this magical thing they were sharing had a future. She was just amazed that they should be kissing at all and that she'd so longed for it without even knowing why.

'I've never kissed anyone as amazing as you,' Rafe murmured much later, when they'd slowly, reluctantly drawn apart.

'Or not recently?' Toni teased softly, reluctant to accept his compliment. She didn't know why. 'You're pretty amazing yourself.'

'So, I take it we're both pretty amazing.' His eyes gleamed with humour.

Toni laughed shakily. This was dangerous ground. Scary.

She took a little step back from him. 'Are we going to have that swim, then?'

'We'd better, I think.' His mouth brushed hers again. And again. 'Otherwise I'm going to need a cold shower.'

They swam, stroking lazily up and down the pool. Then they floated. Blinking the droplets from her eyes, Toni looked up into the blueness of a summer sky—it was beautiful, vast. A feeling of pure gladness twisted inside her.

The beauty of the world, her world, was all around them. Rafe was barely an arm's length away and nothing had ever felt so right. Suddenly she wanted to share everything with him. The sky, the cool depths of the water, the musky perfume of the jasmine and the other more elusive smells that charged her senses.

'Rafe?' Scooping her hand into the water, she shot a spray of droplets on to his chest. 'Open your eyes.'

'They're open.'

'Look up. What do you see?' she asked, her voice hushed with expectancy.

'Blue sky,' he said without inflection. 'And more blue sky.'

'That's pathetic!' Toni showered him with water again. 'Where's your imagination, Riccardi!'

That was too much for Rafe. He made a lunge at her but she was too quick, stroking away from him. However, her stroke was no match for his long arms. He caught up to her quickly. Toni screamed her protest as he ducked her but she bobbed up in a second slicked with water, her hands clasped around his neck. Laughingly, they kissed playfully, once, twice.

Just when it changed into something else, Toni wasn't sure. Holding her gaze with an intensity that rocked her to the core, Rafe laid his open palm across her bare midriff. Then, bending his head, he kissed the soft swell of her breast above her bikini top.

'Rafe…' A jagged breath left Toni's mouth. Lifting her hands, she slid them down the wet sleekness of his naked back and he dragged in a huge breath and lifted his head.

'Out, I think, Antonia.' His voice was clogged and he shook the water from his hair. Towing her to the end of the pool, he hoisted her up the ladder.

'Coming?' Toni looked back over her shoulder.

'I need a minute.' His grin was rueful. 'Go, get your shower.'

Toni fled as if she'd been stung.

Stripping off her bikini, she threw herself into the shower, letting it run full pelt. She used Rafe's soap. Nice, she decided, lathering it and letting the bubbles run off her skin. She picked up his bottle of shampoo and let some nestle in the palm of her hand. It smelled nice too. As she shampooed her hair and rinsed it, her thoughts came to a dead end.

Were they playing games again? She bit the softness of her lower lip, turning off the water and reaching for a towel. Towels, she corrected. She'd need an extra one to dry her hair. She blinked a bit, seeing two pristine white towels hanging neatly on the rail. Obviously, he'd put them there. For her. He'd thought of the possibility of them swimming. Well, she had as well. Suddenly, she gave a shaky little laugh. Oh, Rafe... There was so much to love about him. *Like*, she amended quickly, and wrapping her body in one of the towels and her hair in the other, she tip-toed through to his bedroom.

As she dressed, she could hear the cicadas tick, tick, ticking outside in the shrubbery, feel the warm press of air, because he hadn't switched on the air-conditioning in the bedroom. The softest smile touched her mouth. I could make love with him right here, right now. And it would feel so perfect. But there was so much she didn't know about him. Would she ever get the chance?

She finished blotting her hair and, somewhat more composed, she made her way back outside to the courtyard. Rafe was still there. He was sitting forward on the chair, hands linked across his knees, looking across the pool to the enclosed tennis court beyond.

'Shower's free,' she said, taking the other chair beside him.

'Joe and Cath have a great set-up here,' he said quietly.

Toni sent him a sharp look. There'd been almost longing in his voice. 'I guess when you have to bring up five kids in a country town, you have to go all out to keep them entertained,' she said.

'I hope they enjoy Italy.'

'Oh, they will.' Toni was enthusiastic. 'My parents took

me to France for a year when I was fifteen. It was magic.
And Marcus, their eldest, is seventeen. He'll so enjoy the
experience of living in another country, as will Rosie and
Madeleine. Even the two little ones will have a ball.'

'You know the family well?'

'Mmm. Spent lots of time here. I helped Cath now and
again with her fundraising for the school.'

Rafe looked thoughtful, lying back in his chair. 'How
do you raise such a big family these days?'

Toni shrugged. 'Like Joe and Cath do, I guess. With
plenty of imagination, a few ground rules and a good dose
of love thrown in.'

She made it sound so easy. He expelled a hard breath
and rubbed his hands back through his hair. 'I'll get that
shower.' He hoisted himself to his feet. 'Make yourself
at home.'

'Oh, I am.' Toni twinkled a smile up at him and wig-
gled her bare toes.

In the shower, Rafe lathered himself, letting the warm
jet of water spray over his head and slick down over his
shoulders to puddle round his feet.

He had to lighten up.

He'd think of Antonia. That should work. She continued to amaze him, startle him out of his prosaic routine
of thinking, of acting. But he hadn't shaped up too badly
today, he thought. Along with the lady herself, he decided
they'd done pretty well for a first date. If that's what it
was. Conversationally, there hadn't been any awkward
pauses and they'd disclosed a little of their personal lives
to one another.

And they'd kissed. He couldn't, *wouldn't* forget that.

Towelling himself dry, he pulled on washed-out jeans
and a black T-shirt, and wandered outside to join Toni. He
opened the door to the annexe and paused. She was still

sitting there, looking as relaxed as a small, boneless cat. He noticed the afternoon sun was beginning to lose some of its heat and a breeze had begun to make snake-like ripples across the pool. 'Glass of wine?' he asked.

Toni looked back at him and smiled. 'Oh, yes, please. Could you bring it out? I don't feel like moving yet.'

Rafe merely raised an eyebrow. 'My pleasure,' he said. And it was, he told himself, all the way to the fridge and back again. It surely was.

Toni took her first sip of the wine. 'It's lovely.'

'I'm a bit out of the loop with choosing wine. This seems to have won a major award, though, so it should be all right.'

'It's gorgeous.' Toni relaxed back into the chair. It had been a very eventful day. But instead of feeling fatigued, she felt strangely exhilarated. And she didn't want it to end. She turned to Rafe. 'Would you like me to make us an early dinner or would you rather I took myself off?'

He reached across and took her hand, sliding his fingers through hers. 'Now, isn't that a loaded question, Antonia?' He gave her fingers a little more pressure. 'What do you think I'd want?'

His statement was enough to reignite the tension that had been lashing the air between them since their wild interaction in the pool. Toni's heartbeat revved. 'I think you'd like me to make dinner, Rafe. That's what I think.'

'And you'd be right.' He gave an off-key laugh and pressed her hand briefly to his mouth.

'Let's finish our drinks, then I'll get started.' Toni gently took back her hand. 'What do you have in by way of food? In other words, what possibilities do I have?'

He chuckled. 'If you're trying to catch me out, Ms Morell, I'm sorry to disappoint you. Cath left a heap of dry goods in the pantry and I did a shop for perishables on Thursday night.'

Toni smiled. 'So we're in business?'

'Yep.' He smiled back. 'We're in business.'

'OK, let's see what we have to work with here.' Toni did a quick inventory of the contents of the pantry and what she saw delighted her. 'There's canned tomatoes, spices and dried pasta. So if you have sweet potatoes in your crisper I can make us a feast.'

'I threw in all kinds of fruit and veg at the supermarket,' Rafe said. 'There's bound to be spuds of some kind.' He went to look. 'We're in luck.' He drew out two large sweet potatoes and laid them on the bench. 'What else do you need?'

'Parmesan cheese?'

'I have that.'

'Excellent. Then I'll just nip round to Cath's herb garden for some oregano and we're set.'

Watching indulgently as Toni prepared the meal, Rafe said, 'You really do know your way around the kitchen.'

Toni showed him the tip of her tongue. 'You thought I was just a spoilt little rich girl?'

He sobered. 'I've seen how brilliantly you run a busy casualty department, Antonia. I'd never think of you as that.'

She blushed a little at his compliment, turning to the stove to give the bubbling pasta a final twirl with her fork. 'Nearly there,' she said. 'And we'll need some large bowls.'

'I think I can manage that.' Rafe went to the wall cupboard, found the bowls and set them down on the table. 'We should have some authentic Italian music to accompany our meal.'

Toni turned from the stove. 'I'm surprised you don't have some.'

He shrugged. 'I only brought the basics with me to Forrestdale. The bulk of my stuff is at my parents' place.'

'Perhaps you could sing,' Toni deadpanned.

He chuckled. 'Perhaps I could—but I won't.'

They ate with obvious enjoyment. 'How did I do, then?' Toni sent him an arch little look.

'You did so well I might just keep you.' His gaze shimmered over her face and then roamed to register the gleam of lamplight in her hair and on the ridge of her collarbone. Hells bells, he could almost taste her... 'More wine?'

'No, one's my limit, thanks,' she said, feeling happy and fizzy inside. She wound pasta around her fork. 'So, why Doctors without Borders?'

His shoulders tensed slightly. He'd expected this question eventually. But how much or how little to tell her? 'Why not?' he prevaricated.

'It would seem an enormous decision to make,' Toni said practically. 'An interruption to your career path. So I'm guessing you had a pretty good reason.'

Oh, he'd had a good reason, all right. Rafe's mouth tightened fractionally. 'I went along to an MSF information evening. They were recruiting. What I saw inspired me. There's a saying about the needs being great but the labourers being few—or something like that. I signed on and after orientation, I was appointed to Seim Reap, a city in north-western Cambodia. Our hospital dealt mainly with children.'

So, treating desperately sick kids day in day out must surely have affected him, Toni thought. Was that the reason for the shadow behind his eyes sometimes? 'You've mentioned malnourishment. What other kinds of problems did you treat?'

'Dengue fever, malaria and school sores were high on the agenda. But pneumonia and diarrhoea are right up there as potential killers as well. We saw a lot of kids from the surrounding villages. The mothers used to make quite long journeys to bring them in. Sometimes they'd have to line up all day just to get seen.'

Toni shook her head. 'We don't have much to complain about here, then, do we?'

'We expect more. Demand more from our health system most probably. Whereas those folk were just grateful to be seen at all.'

Toni picked up the glass of water beside her plate and took a mouthful. She felt a wall of questions unanswered but how far could she go without invading his privacy? As far as he'd let her, she thought philosophically. She drummed up a smile. 'So, is it good to be home?'

Rafe considered his answer. Much about it was good, he had to admit. Meeting Antonia herself was good—better than good. And if he hadn't yet come to terms with the complex reasons why he'd gone in the first place, well, so be it...

'I'm on leave,' he said, neatly evading a direct answer. 'It's mandatory after a year.' It wasn't but he couldn't tell her about the PTSD. And that he'd been *ordered* to take leave.

That sounded like he was going back. Toni resumed eating. And if that didn't throw out warning flags to pull back before she went in boots and all again, nothing would.

But her heart wasn't listening.

By mutual, silent consent, they finished the meal talking about everything and nothing. 'Now I'm going to help you with the washing-up and then take my leave,' Toni said, getting up from the table.

'There's a perfectly good dishwasher,' Rafe countered. 'You're not here to skivvy for me.'

'Fine.' Toni got to her feet. 'I'll just grab my bag.' She walked along the hallway to his bedroom, collected her bag from the chair and came back.

'All set?' His attempt at a smile faded. 'I'll walk you out.' When they got to her car, he stopped and held her briefly. 'Thanks for today.'

'I had a lovely time,' she said softly. 'Did you?'

'Yes, it was a good day,' he answered shortly.

Toni blinked uncertainly. His response had sounded almost as detached, as if they'd done a great job weeding the garden. She hesitated, catching the flicker of something in his eyes under the streetlamp, and for a split second he swayed towards her. Not far enough to kiss her but...

'Well, goodnight,' he said.

Toni needed no second invitation. Using her keypad to unlock the door, she slipped into the driver's seat and started the engine. In seconds, she was purring away.

Well, that was all a bit odd at the end, she mused as she drove. There'd been no little intimate farewell to acknowledge the very special day they'd had. Just—shut down. She sighed. The evening had all gone downhill after she'd asked him about his time with MSF. And he'd never really explained why he'd joined them in the first place. Well, let him keep his secrets. But whatever they were, they sure didn't make him happy.

Rafe thumped the control on the dishwasher to start the cycle. 'Idiot!' he muttered through clenched teeth. It had been the best day of his life for as long as he could remember. *The best day.* So, why had he let it end so crappily? Antonia must think he was the worst kind of jerk.

In a gesture of a man almost at the end of his tether, he raised his hands, ploughing his fingers through his hair and locking them at the back of his neck. He'd make it up to her. Just how, he didn't know yet.

Sunday morning.

Toni woke with a new purpose. She showered and dressed in shorts and a loose-fitting top and went to make breakfast. Life had to be lived, she'd decided. She wasn't going to over-analyse things where Rafe was concerned. She more than liked his company and she guessed he didn't find her too repulsive. They were adults. They could mix pleasure with working together. Surely that wasn't too difficult?

She took her breakfast outside to the pergola in her back garden. As she ate, she smiled at the busyness of the small-bird population. There were wagtails in abundance, switching their little tails from side to side as they snapped up insects from the lawn.

Seeing the birds so involved about their day, Toni thought of what to do with her own day. A few possibilities entered her head, one of which sent her indoors to the phone. Rafe picked up on the second ring.

'Riccardi.'

'Hi, it's me…'

'Hi, me.' His voice was suddenly eager. 'What can I do for you?'

'Ah—do you play tennis by any chance?'

'I can play a bit. We had a light plane strip next to the hospital in Seam Reip, which doubled as a court. Now and again we got the chance to down tools and enjoy a game or two. So, do you want to come over for a hit?'

'In a while.' She didn't want to appear too keen. 'I've a few things to do first.'

'And I want to run over to the hospital and check on Simone so can we say in an hour, then?'

'Suits me.'

'Fine. Look forward to it. And, Antonia?' He hesitated.

'Something else?'

'Just…thanks.'

Toni rolled her eyes at the inanimate instrument and hung up.

'The tennis net's in the garden shed,' Toni said when she arrived. 'I'll help you put it up. There are some racquets as well, although I have my own with me.'

'You play regularly, then?' Rafe asked as they made their way along the path.

'Thursday nights at the sports ground. You're welcome to come along any time. It's a friendly crowd.'

His mouth flickered in a controlled smile. 'Thanks for the invitation.'

Between them, they erected the net across the court and took their places at either end. Rafe looked on admiringly, watching as Toni executed a few light gym exercises. Turning away, he did his own warm-up of a few stretches against the steel-framed fence.

'Ready?' she called, sending him a sweetly innocent smile.

Rafe acknowledged her call with a lift of his hand. And then it was game on.

Shrugging off the loss of the first two games, Toni consoled herself that she was just getting her eye in. But Rafe was good, she allowed. Strong and purposeful.

At his end of the court, Rafe alternated his feet rhythmically on the spot and watched for Toni's first service. He could tell already she was a precise player, fast and deadly accurate. And those legs! Poetry in motion. Concentrate, Riccardi, he warned himself. This lady is no push-over.

Taking a moment to gather herself, Toni rocketed her first service in, the ball kicking up the chalk as it ripped past Rafe. Just out. He raised his racquet in acknowledgment, narrowing his eyes in concentration.

Game after game, they tested one another, both sweating with exertion, the score see-sawing until Toni had the advantage, the longed-for chance of clinching the game and set.

Pulling back, she struck the ball, a low grunt of satisfaction accompanying its speedy passage straight past him. Bemusedly, Rafe watched the ball's trajectory and shook his head. 'You aced me!'

'So I did.' Slightly breathless, laughing, Toni ran up to the net. 'Game and set to me, I think. Shake?'

'What about another set to prove your point?' Rafe enclosed her smaller hand in his. 'Don't I get the chance to break even?'

'Uh-uh.' Toni shook her head, puffing the tiny tendrils off her forehead. 'We'll have to make time for a rematch.'

'You'd better believe it,' he growled, marching her off the court and back to the annexe.

Laughing, Toni prodded him in the ribs. 'Not a sore loser, are you, Dr Riccardi?'

He gave a rueful grin. 'Just a tad humiliated. You really can play, can't you?'

'I made the finals of the state junior hard court titles when I was sixteen. And we have a court at home. Dad and I played a lot.'

A dry smile tugged his mouth. 'I guess I should be grateful I lost by only one point, then?'

Wrinkling her nose at him, Toni settled on one of the outdoor chairs in the courtyard. 'Any cool drinks on offer?'

'I'll get some juice.' Rafe went inside, returning with jug

and glasses. 'This'll quench your thirst,' he said, pouring the liquid into the glasses. He handed one across to her.

'Oh, yes!' she said and licked her lips. 'That is so good. How is Simone?' Toni asked, as they drank slowly.

'Happier when she's allowed to have a shower.' He chuckled. 'Keith will let her home as soon as it's practical. She'll need to rest up, which is not making her too thrilled. She was supposed to go to her uni orientation day next week.'

'With care, she might be able to get there,' Toni said. 'Poor kid.'

'Thank heaven her parents were with her,' Rafe spoke with feeling.

'Thank heaven *you* were with her,' Toni countered.

A long beat of silence.

Rafe cleared his throat. 'Sorry I went weird on you last night.'

Toni's shoulders lifted in a shrug. 'It's OK.'

'No, it's not OK.' He shook his head. 'You gave up your Saturday to show me around the place. And it was magic.' His look softened. '*You* were magic.'

Toni blushed gently. 'I had fun too.' She paused. 'You seemed to withdraw a bit after I asked about the reasons you went to work for MSF. There has to be more than you're telling me. More than just going to a *talk*.' She stopped. 'I respect your privacy but sometimes it's just good to let it out…'

Rafe's breath came out on a sigh. 'I wanted to tell you…'

Toni held his gaze steadily. 'You've been hurt, haven't you?'

He tipped his head back and blew out a controlling breath. 'When I said I went to a talk, I should have said, we—my wife and I.'

'You're married!' Shocked into disbelief, Toni could only stare at him. Not this. She shook her head. Not again.

'*Was*,' he emphasised. 'We're divorced.'

Toni swallowed past the constriction in her throat. 'What happened?'

Another long beat of silence.

'We'd been married for six months. Going to work for one of the aid agencies was something we'd both always wanted to do. So we signed on.'

'She was a doctor too?'

'Yes.' His face was carefully expressionless. 'Gabrielle was training towards a specialty in paeds.'

Toni gave a sharp glance at the sudden tight set of his shoulders. 'So, working in a children's hospital would have fitted into her plans.'

'You'd have thought so. But a week after we'd signed, she told me she couldn't go.' He hesitated infinitesimally. 'Needless to say, I was stunned. I said I'd withdraw but she said I should go—in fact, I *needed* to go.'

'Was there no room for compromise?' Toni asked guardedly. 'I mean, could you both have gone for a shorter time?'

He shook his head. 'I asked what her reasons were for pulling out, I demanded them, in fact. It wasn't pretty. She finally broke down and told me she wanted out of the marriage. That she'd met someone else.'

Toni sat up straight. 'That's awful, Rafe! You must have been gutted.'

'Yep.' His mouth moved into a twist of a grim smile. 'The really obscene part was that it started on our wedding day. Or should I say started again.'

Toni made a sound of distress in her throat. What kind of a woman had he married, for heaven's sake?

'He was someone from her past. A lawyer. He'd been practising in the States. Their parents were best buddies,' he added bitterly. 'When he arrived back unexpectedly several days before the wedding, Gabrielle's mother invited him along. She didn't tell her daughter. But there he was, as large as life, when we walked down the aisle, grinning at her like a bloody banshee.'

Toni frowned a bit. She'd thought banshees wailed, not grinned, but that was beside the point. 'What happened then?'

His shoulders moved in a tight shrug. 'He, Michael, monopolised her for the entire reception. She hardly talked to our other guests.'

'Did you not sense something was wrong?'

He snorted. 'You bet I did. I took him aside and told him to leave quietly or I'd help him out the door. Gabby and I had a short honeymoon and things seemed…all right. And then we were both busy in our jobs. I was doing my final part surgery so I was pushed, a bit jaded. I hadn't really noticed she'd been pulling away until she spelled it out.' He laughed, a harsh, angry sound. 'And that was that. I filed for divorce, deferred MSF and went to work for the Flying Doctors. When the divorce was through, I went to Cambodia. Gabrielle eventually married the banshee.'

Toni felt at a loss for words but finally came up with, 'I can imagine how angry you must have felt.'

'Oh, yes, I felt angry. And *conned*.'

'I know how that feels.' Toni gave a hard-edged laugh. Briefly, she told him about her affair with Alex.

A soft oath left his mouth. 'How could he have done that to you?'

Toni brought her head up. 'I don't still have feelings for him, if that's what you're thinking. It just galls me sometimes to realise I gave so much to the relationship and it was all built on sand. But it's history now, as they say.' She got to her feet. 'My laundry's not going to do itself, so I'm going to run. Thanks for the drink and the game of tennis.'

Rafe rose as well. Without thinking, he reached out and his arms went around her. 'I wish you didn't have to go…' This time it was his eyes that were filled with longing.

Toni steeled herself. It would so easy to just forget everything and go to bed with him. But at the moment that was a bridge too far. 'That's not a good idea, Rafe. You need to heal.'

His mouth turned down. 'Maybe I am healed.'

And maybe he was using her as a lifeline. She wasn't about to leave herself open for that. Not again. She gently pulled away. 'See you tomorrow.'

CHAPTER SEVEN

TONI'S heart was all but leaping against her chest wall as
she drove to work next morning. She'd spent half the night
trying to get Rafe out of her head but he wouldn't go. She
just hoped he hadn't had second thoughts about confid-
ing in her. But if he turned all awkward with her, well, she
wasn't having it. Not for a second.

But she need not have worried. Rafe was brisk and professional, whisking her into his office the moment she'd
arrived in the department. 'We have a problem,' he said,
pointing her to a chair and dropping into his own. Having
gained Toni's attention, he went on, 'Three more toddlers
have presented with vomiting and diarrhoea, one had to
be admitted. All from the caravan park.'

Toni went still. 'That's very serious. We'll obviously
have to move fast before we have a full-scale epidemic on
our hands.' Or a tragedy, she added silently, a sick feeling
beginning to shred the nerves in her stomach.

'I've already been on to Bernie Maguire,' Rafe said.
'He's had someone making discreet enquiries on general
conditions at the caravan park.' His mouth drew in. 'It's
not looking good.'

'Joanne Carter mentioned the manager was the pits,
do you recall?'

Rafe nodded. 'At this stage we can only assume the

infection is coming from the water. But it's tank water,'
he emphasised. 'Apparently, the manager, Tyler Bendix,
decided the council water rates were too high and cutting
into his profits, so he installed tanks. God alone knows
where the water has come from.'

'That's appalling, Rafe. Let's get cracking and get over
there, demand he give us a sample of water for testing—'

'Steady on, Antonia.' He raised a staying hand. 'We
have to follow protocol.'

'Meanwhile toddlers are falling ill all over the place!'
Toni was outraged. 'It's not good enough, Rafe!'

'I know that.' He was patient. 'As acting health officer
for the place, I'm about to go over to the council offices
now. They have ultimate jurisdiction for the regulations
at the caravan park so it'll have to be someone from their
community health team who has the authority to get the
sample.'

Toni half rose. 'I'll come with you.'

'Good.' Rafe swung to his feet. 'I'd hoped you'd want
to.'

As they drove uptown to the council offices, Rafe asked,
'You seem to know everyone in the place. Do you know
this Mary Gilchrist we have to see?'

'Mmm. She's been an alderman for a couple of years,
former nurse. She'll know how to get things moving.'

Mary Gilchrist came out of her office to greet them. She
was in her early fifties, her blonde-grey hair smartly styled
into a sharp bob, her manner professional but friendly.
'Toni, hello.' Her smile was warm.

Toni returned her greeting. 'Mary, this is Dr Rafe
Riccardi. He's acting health officer while Dr Lyons is
away.'

'Dr Riccardi.' Mary held out her hand. 'I believe this a
matter of some urgency you've come about?'

'It is, Mrs Gilchrist,' Rafe said. 'We'd appreciate your help.'

Mary ushered them into her office. When they were seated, Rafe gave brief, succinct facts as they knew them.

'So, you see, we really need to sort this before things get out of hand,' Toni added earnestly.

'Oh, indeed,' Mary agreed. 'As you probably know, all health matters pertaining to caravan parks come under the council's banner, so let's see what further information we can find out about Mr Bendix, shall we?' She began running information through on her computer screen. 'Ah! According to what we have here, this gentleman doesn't actually own the park. He's the appointed manager of a company called Gretel Holdings.'

'So…' Rafe exchanged a quick look with Toni. 'Tyler Bendix has taken it upon himself to make these changes.'

'Logically, we could assume that,' Mary was guarded. 'I'll get one of our officers over there smartly to take a sample of the tank water. But I'm afraid it'll have to go to Sydney for testing. It's a rather involved process.'

'Immunomagnetic separation,' Rafe supplied quietly.

Mary raised a well-defined brow. 'You know about it, Doctor?'

He gave a tight smile. 'I've been working in Cambodia.'

'Ah.' Mary's little nod, acknowledged the significance of his words. 'Then you'd be well acquainted with what we may be up against.'

'To save time and negate the possibility of more children going down, we could do a very preliminary analysis here,' Rafe offered.

Toni spun him a wide-eyed searching look. 'The slide-under-the-microscope technique?'

He shrugged. 'How's your science?'

'A-plus. I have enough to know what to look for,' she said shortly.

Slightly bemused, Mary Gilchrist looked from one to the other. 'As long as you feel capable of getting some answers…?'

'The test may be elementary,' Rafe allowed, 'but it will certainly tell us if there are bugs in the water. We had scare after scare when I was working overseas. Initially we did our own very basic sampling so we could act to minimise the risks to people's health. A proper breakdown will have to be left to the lab, of course,' he allowed.

'Naturally. But let's get the ball rolling, shall we?' Mary picked up the phone. 'You'll have your sample within the hour.'

'Thanks, Mary.' Rafe stuck out his hand. 'Ask your officer to deliver it to me personally, would you, please? My office is on the ground floor. We'll get back to you as soon as we have anything to report.'

But an hour passed and then another and there was still no water sample. And another young child had been admitted with the same severe symptoms.

Toni was worried. To stave off wild alarm, she couldn't tell any of her staff, not even Liz.

'You're like a cat on the proverbial tin roof,' Liz remarked. 'What's up?'

Toni flapped a hand. 'Internal matter. I'll put you in the picture as soon as I can, Lizzie.'

'I've hardly seen you all morning.' Liz's brows rose interrogatively. 'Nice weekend?'

'Mmm, lovely,' Toni responded absently. And then, because she just had to tell someone, she blurted out, 'Rafe wanted to see something of the district so I acted as his guide. We went over to Maeburn.'

'Wow! You dark filly!'

'We had a swim at his place too. And a game of tennis.'

'Wow, again!' Liz's gaze narrowed. 'I thought you looked a bit dreamy earlier.'

Toni scoffed. 'I've never looked dreamy in my life!'

'Well…' Liz thought for a minute. 'Expectant, then.'

'Oh, lord, Lizzie! Don't use that word around me. Please!'

'My stars!' Liz's blue eyes gleamed. 'You slept with him!'

'I did not! And when you've quite finished writing this ridiculous script of my life, perhaps you'd check if Friday's bloods have come back.'

'Antonia, could you—?' Rafe popped his head in at the station. Seeing Liz, he stopped abruptly. 'Could you give me a minute, please?'

'Certainly.' Toni looked a warning at Liz before departing. All she heard in return was Liz's throaty chuckle.

Rafe stopped when they were out of earshot. 'The water sample's here,' he said. 'Finally.'

'What was the hold-up? I was beginning to wonder.'

His jaw tightened. 'Our man Bendix wouldn't allow the council officer onto the premises. He had to get a court order.'

'That just proves he's as guilty as sin,' Toni asserted with the air of a kitten about to turn into a tiger. 'Where do you want to do this testing?'

'We'll use the facilities in X-Ray,' Rafe said. 'We'll do it now while the techs are on a break.'

'It's all a bit clandestine, isn't it?' Toni said grimly.

'Can't be helped. We don't want the dogs barking before we've something tangible to go on.'

It took only seconds to set up their respective microscopes and slides. And only a few seconds more to own their worse fears were now realities.

'Sweet God…' Rafe muttered, his gaze narrowing into the lens. 'If this water's ever seen the inside of a filtering plant, I'll shout all the shifts' free booze for a month.'

'Oh, Rafe…this is sickening.' Toni homed in on her own sample. 'This has to be seething with pollutants.'

'And breeding lovely bugs like cryptosporidium and giardia,' he growled. 'And heaven knows what else.'

Toni's stomach felt hollowed out at the implications. 'Giardia can take months to be eradicated from the system, can't it?'

'Try *years,*' Refe affirmed grimly.

Toni met his gaze fearfully. 'What about the families who have left the park and who might have consumed some of the water? They'll need to be contacted urgently.'

'We'll have to find them first.' Rafe's expression became tight. 'But from what I gathered from Bernie, the tanks were installed very recently. So with a bit of luck we may have caught it in time. But it'll have to be a matter for the police now. So let's not hang about here. Mary will be waiting for our findings.'

'Then do it now, Rafe.' Toni practically pushed him out the door. 'I'll clear up here.'

He was just putting the phone down when she caught up with him in his office. 'What's happening?' She slid into a chair and faced him across his desk.

'The council is organising crates of bottled water to be trucked over to the park as we speak. The residents will have to keep using that until things can be sorted.'

'And the park manager?'

'It's out of our hands. Mary's informed the police. They'll do a door-knock around the park residents and tell them what's going on. If the law's been broken, the police are the ones with the authority to lay charges.'

'Good.' Toni nodded her satisfaction. 'And, hey, well done, you!'

Rafe smiled a little crookedly. 'Well done, us, I think.'

There was a heightened buzz in the staffroom next morning as the early shift caught up about what had happened at the caravan park. This time Rafe sat among them, relaxed over his mug of green tea.

'So, what's happened about this Bendix guy?' Ed wanted to know.

Rafe's mouth turned down. 'He's done a runner.'

'No!' Liz was outraged. 'How come?'

'As soon as the council people came with authority to collect a water sample, he guessed the game was up and he scarpered.'

'Will they find him?' Amy asked, wide-eyed at the drama.

'Let's hope so. According to Bernie Maguire, the police put out an APB pretty quickly.'

Harmony looked blank. 'What's an APB?'

'All-points bulletin,' Ed, who was a devotee of police TV shows, said knowledgeably. 'And if he's driving that clapped-out yellow wagon, they'll spot him a mile off.'

Toni, who had remained silent, absorbing with something like pleasure Rafe's relaxed interaction with the team, asked, 'So, what's the water situation now at the park? Do we know?'

Rafe's gaze went to her mouth and lingered. 'The town water was reconnected last night. The park residents are safe again.'

'Oh, man,' Ed said, serious for once. 'Lucky you spotted it, Doc.'

'Right place at the right time.' Rafe shrugged off the compliment.

'Now, while we're all here…'Liz gained everyone's attention with a ting-ting on the side of her empty coffee mug. 'My granddad, Tom Marchant, turns eighty on Saturday. He's invited half the district out to his place so if any of you feel like a day out in the bush, you're most welcome to come along.'

'Old Tom is eighty?' Ed marvelled. 'He doesn't look it. He's as fit as.'

'That's what he'd have us believe,' Liz said dryly. 'Anyway, Granddad's place is called Blue Hills and it's about twenty Ks out of town on North Road. The creek's there and it's safe for the kids to swim or paddle and Tom'll have his ponies around to give them rides.'

'Well, I for one would love to come,' Mel, single mum of two, who lived in a flat in town, said quietly. 'My boys would relish getting out in the bush.'

'I'll have to pass.' Amy looked crestfallen. 'I swapped shifts with Dayle Burton. She's got a wedding on.'

'Not to worry, Ames. I'll keep you some birthday cake,' Liz promised.

'Speaking of food, what can we bring?' someone else asked.

'Just yourselves,' Liz said firmly. 'We're doing a barbecue. And, Rafe…' she tilted an arch smile at the senior registrar '…might be a nice chance for you to see a bit *more* of our district.'

'Thanks, Liz.' Rafe gave a slight bow of his head in acknowledgment. 'I'd appreciate that. I'll do my best to be there. Antonia has already given me a tour of Maeburn. It was amazing.'

A few curious eyes swung in Toni's direction and she flashed Liz a *thanks-for-nothing* look. And then smiled with mock-sweetness. 'What time do you want us, Lizzie?'

Liz gave an open-handed shrug. 'Wander out whenever and stay as long as you like.'

The week sped by. Conscious of speculative looks her way, Toni kept her interaction with Rafe to a minimum. She'd become quite good at that, she decided, and then wondered why she cared if the staff knew about her and Rafe. What was there to know anyway? she rationalised. He was keeping out of her way as well. Were they both being ridiculous? Probably.

Buoyed up by this train of thought, she sped along to his office at the end of her shift on Friday afternoon. She knocked and popped her head in. 'Got a minute?'

He waved her in. 'I won't keep you,' Toni said, placing her hands across the back of a chair.

He sent her a lazy smile. 'I'm happy to be *kept*.'

She rolled her eyes. 'I'm just wondering if you're still coming out to Tom Marchant's do tomorrow?'

Rafe pulled himself upright. 'I thought perhaps we could go together.'

Toni's heart jolted under her ribs. 'You realise we'd probably be an *item* by midday?'

'Let's give 'em their money's worth, then.' He flashed her a grin. 'Tell me where you live and I'll pick you up.'

Toni bit her lip. 'Are you sure about this, Rafe?'

'Aren't you?' he flung back.

Toni felt her need to spend time with him widen to a river. 'I'd love it,' she said simply.

On Saturday morning, Toni was ready early. Her spirits felt light. She was spending the day with Rafe. Smiling, she did a little twirl in front of the mirror. She felt cool and chic in white cotton pants and a white shirt with a pinstripe of lime green. A floppy sun hat was already in her bag.

She spun from the mirror when a rap sounded on her front door. It seemed Rafe was early too. She almost skipped to let him in.

'All set?' His grin was infectious Toni found as she grinned back at him.

She beckoned him in. 'I'll just get my bag.'

'Wait,' he said softly. He leaned forward, putting his hands to her elbows, smoothing them up inside the sleeves of her shirt to enclose her upper arms. 'Good morning...'

A jagged breath left Toni's mouth. She felt her skin prickle and then contract. Lifting her hands to the back of his neck, she gusted a tiny sound of release and drew his face down to hers.

And when they kissed, she felt renewed all over again. Brand new and sparkling.

'Antonia...you're beautiful...' Pulling back, Rafe buried his face in her throat, his hands sliding beneath her shirt to roam restlessly across her back and then to her midriff, half circling her ribcage, smoothing upwards until his thumbs stroked the soft underswell of her breasts.

They kissed again and with a passion she hardly knew she possessed she kissed him back, opening her mouth on his, inviting him into all her secret places, tasting him all over again.

'We could skip the party...'

Rafe's meaning was clear and Toni felt a fluttering inside, her mind zeroing in on the fact that they were alone and there was no one here to disturb them. Whatever they chose to do...

'I want to be with you, Antonia...' His hands stroked up her arms before he gathered her in again, holding her to him so that she felt the imprint of him from thigh to breast.

'Rafe...' She drew in a small breath, feeling his hands

on her lower back, tilting her closer still and the sweet sting of anticipation slithered up her spine.

'Just say the word.' His voice was muffled against her hair.

Toni took a breath so deep it almost hurt. Could she? Dare she? Winding her arms around his neck, she closed her eyes picturing him as her lover, dreaming of his body claiming hers completely, fully.

Honestly.

And when he took her mouth again, the feeling of oneness was so intense, so tangible she almost gave the answer he wanted to hear. But a little voice in her head kept insisting that once they'd taken that step, there was no going back. Nothing would be simple between them again.

Nothing.

Wordlessly, she stepped away from him. Wrapping her arms around her midriff, she shook her head slowly. 'It's not that I don't want you too. But I can't take this lightly, Rafe.'

'Are you saying I am?'

She looked at him squarely. 'No, I'm not saying that. But there's a thousand reasons why we shouldn't go rushing into things.'

He made a sound of dissension in his throat and turned away.

'You're vulnerable, Rafe.'

Toni's bald statement had him turning back and tilting his head towards her. 'Perhaps it's you who's vulnerable, Antonia.'

She threw up her hands. 'All right! Perhaps we both are. We trusted people and they let us down. It would be so easy to let things get complicated between us.'

His throat moved convulsively as he swallowed. He speared his hands into the back pockets of his cargos.

'You're probably right,' he conceded, a note of apology in his voice. 'I appreciate what we have. Don't look like that,' he said soothingly, 'or everyone will think we've had a row.'

She managed a token smile. 'We can't have that and spoil their matchmaking.'

He gave a click of annoyance. 'I'd almost forgotten how lethal hospital gossip can be.' His mouth kicked up in a crooked smile. 'Friends again?'

'Of course.'

'Go, get your stuff, then, and we'll make tracks.'

'Hang on a tick.' Toni reached into her pocket for a tissue. 'You're wearing a trace of my lipstick. There,' she blotted his mouth expertly. 'Not even Liz would suspect anything.'

'So, tell me about granddad Tom,' Rafe said as they began their journey to Blue Hills.

Toni relaxed. This was safe ground. 'He was born and bred here, one of the most respected seniors in the district. Tom's an amazing old chap, one of nature's gentlemen, as my mother would say. He and his late wife Jeannie were champion equestrians in their younger days. That's probably why he's kept his interest in the ponies.

'For years he and Jeannie conducted a riding school for differently abled children. They even had several little cottages built on their farm so the parents could stay and make it a kind of holiday. And they never accepted any payment. Just asked the parents to do their own catering.'

'That's remarkable.' Rafe was clearly impressed. 'Kindness in any form can't be measured, can it?'

'I'm so glad you feel like that.'

'Why wouldn't I?' He jerked a shoulder self-deprecatingly.

Toni chose to ignore that question. 'He's Liz's paternal grandfather, by the way. You might have noticed Marchant's Engineering in town? That's Liz's dad Cliff's business. He runs it with her two brothers, Jason and Todd.'

'Sounds like you and Liz go back a way?'

'Liz came to Sydney to do her nurse training. We had our placements together at the Royal North Shore. We clicked almost at once. Became best friends. I was one of her bridesmaids.'

Rafe's mouth tilted. 'One?'

Toni chuckled. 'She had six. Country weddings are inclined to get a bit out of hand, because you daren't leave anyone off the invitation list.' She paused. 'When I'd decided to get out of Sydney, Liz said there was a senior job going here, so I applied and, as luck would have it, I got it.'

'Nothing to do with your outstanding qualifications, I suppose,' Rafe said wryly. 'You seem to have made yourself very much at home here.'

Toni shrugged. 'I enjoy my job. The people are friendly. What's not to like?'

'You don't miss the buzz of the city?'

'Sometimes. But then I can take a break and head back to Sydney. A few days there refreshes me and then I'm more than happy to come back to a more laid-back existence. What about you?'

'I'm enjoying the slower pace here. The hospital is well supported by the board. And not having to scrounge for drugs when you need them is a real bonus.'

'Has working in Cambodia changed you for ever, do you think?'

Oh, boy. That was a loaded question. Rafe's hands tightened on the steering-wheel. 'I'd have to be made of wood if it hadn't.'

Obviously, some deep and meaningful stuff had gone

down there, Toni thought soberly. Stuff he'd maybe rather forget. 'I gather you're not going to take up Matt's offer of a spot on his talk programme, then?'

'No.' His mouth flattened. 'I called him. He was cool about it. I went down that road with a journalist in Seim Reap. She was working for television. She assured she'd be objective and unobtrusive but before I knew it she was dragging stuff out of me about my involvement as a doctor in such a ravaged country. How difficult was it not to let my emotions become involved? Bloody difficult, I should have said, and left it at that. Instead I found myself speechless and shedding tears on camera.' He glanced at Toni, his smile bleak. 'It was heaven-sent footage for the journalist. She was out of there in seconds. She'd got what she wanted.'

'And you were left trying to pick up the pieces,' she surmised softly.

'Something like that.'

'Oh, Rafe… Is that why you took leave?' she asked, hardly daring to breathe.

'I was *told* to take leave.'

Toni bit her lips together. So, he'd been sent home and she wondered why on earth he would even consider going back to a world that seemingly had left him feeling…broken. 'It was a stress issue, then?' she asked carefully.

'So they said. I'm dealing with it. And I'm on *leave*,' he emphasised. 'They haven't booted me out.'

A long beat of silence.

'Rafe, I'm so sorry,' she murmured.

'About what?'

'I was hard on you…judgmental. I had you pegged as an arrogant—'

He gave a throaty laugh. 'Pig.'

'I feel awful now. I was so rude.'

'On the contrary, Antonia.' He found her hand and pressed her knuckles to his lips. 'You were just what I needed.' His eyes turned soft as he glanced at her. 'Still need.'

They lapsed into silence and Toni thought they'd probably given each other a lot to think about. Quite a lot.

'Oh, look,' she said, pointing at the windscreen. 'There's Tom's place up ahead and they've put balloons out to welcome us! I'll bet that was Lizzie's idea.'

Rafe felt his spirits lift. He was glad he'd come. Very glad.

Already, party guests had arrived in droves. There was an air of celebration, of sheer joy at being there to honour Tom Marchant on his eightieth birthday.

'There's Tom.' Toni touched Rafe's arm. 'Come and meet him.'

Toni made the introductions. 'G'day, young fella.' Tom's handshake was firm. 'Liz tells me you've been overseas, working for one of the aid agencies.'

'That's right.' Rafe didn't elaborate.

Tom's blue eyes under his Akubra hat were shrewd and wise. 'So, it must feel good to be back on Aussie soil again, hmm?'

Rafe looked from the slight rise where they were standing down towards the tree-lined creek and then raised his eyes to the ring of blue hills. His nostrils were filled with the scent of the surrounding bush of eucalypts and wild honeysuckle. The clicking of cicadas was ever-present, yet there was a hush that enveloped him, a feeling like no other. His chest lifted in a long breath. 'Yes, it's good to be back. But, hey, today is about you, Mr Marchant. Congratulations on reaching such a milestone.'

Tom gave a wry grin. 'Eighty isn't a bad innings. And

it's Tom, son.' Turning, he reached out an arm and gave Toni a hug. 'How are you, sweetheart?'

'I'm good, thanks, Tom. And happy birthday from me as well.' She gave him a peck on the cheek. 'Thanks for inviting us.'

Tom waved a hand in dismissal. 'This do was all the kids' idea but I guess it's not bad to be remembered on your birthday.'

'What can we do to help?' Rafe asked.

'Just enjoy yourselves,' Tom said. 'But if you must help, young Liz will have a job for you, no doubt.'

They left Tom to greet some of his other guests and made their way towards the house. 'I'll give Ed a hand with the pony rides.' Rafe pointed to where Ed was fast becoming embroiled in kids, bridles and circling ponies.

'Oh, lord.' Toni chuckled. 'Ed is such a *helper.* You'd better rescue him before he maims himself. I'll see what Liz needs. Catch you later?' She smiled up at him.

'If I come out of this alive.' He jogged off.

Toni found Liz in the kitchen. 'Hi, honey, I'm here,' she sing-songed and popped her head around the door.

'Oh, praise be.' Liz indicated a mountain of scones and Australian bush bread, better known as damper. 'All this has to be either slathered with honey or jam and cream. Get stuck in, please, Toni. We're supposed to be serving morning tea in fifteen minutes.'

Toni rolled her eyes. 'Where's your mum? She usually handles this side of things, doesn't she?'

'Still on her way. The bakery was late getting Granddad's birthday cake decorated. Mum's had to hang about. Personally, I think they just plain forgot! Did you bring Rafe?' Liz hopped conversational channels quickly.

'I didn't bring him,' Toni countered. 'We came along together. He's presently helping Ed with the pony rides.'

Liz tutted. 'Todd was supposed to be in charge. Where's he got to?'

Toni laughed softly. 'Actually, he seemed pretty tied up with Mel and her boys.'

'Really? Liz perked up. 'Do we scent a romance in the making?'

'You'd approve, then?'

'Oh, yes. Mel is a real gem and as for Todd—it's about time he got his bachelor butt off the shelf. What about Rafe, though? Will he be safe around the ponies?'

Toni was swiping honey on to the slices of damper. 'His uncle bred racehorses. He told me he learned to ride as a kid.'

Liz gave an arch look. 'So, you've become quite close, then?'

'Yes,' Toni said simply and without embarrassment.

'Oh, Tone...' Liz flashed her friend a sharp look. 'Don't get hurt again, will you?'

'I've my eyes wide open, Lizzie.'

Liz shook her head, cautioning, 'He'll go back, you know?'

Toni spread a crisp tea towel over the food. 'He may not.' And if she honest with herself, she was hanging onto that for all she was worth.

CHAPTER EIGHT

'It's been a great day, hasn't it?' Toni said. Most of the party guests had left and she and Rafe had gone for a walk to the creek. Now they sat under the fringe of a lacy willow that grew along the bank. 'Glad you came?'

'Mmm,' he said lazily, stretching out his legs and making himself comfortable against the trunk of the tree. The day had had a healing quality about it that he couldn't explain. But he was storing up every moment. Holding onto the thought, he closed his eyes, listening to the murmur of the creek mingling with the dozing hum of the cicadas.

Toni snuggled in against him. She would treasure these moments all the days of her life. She felt so in tune with him she could not imagine a time when that could change. Some things were just meant to be.

So engrossed were they with their own thoughts they had no idea of the drama unfolding in the barn, until their names were being called and echoed. And called and echoed.

'That's Liz!' Toni sprang upright. 'I told her we were coming down here. Something must have happened!'

They emerged from under the willow and exploded into a run back up towards the house. Liz came running to meet them.

'It's Granddad! He's fallen, trying to get feed out of the

bin for the ponies. It's tipped forward and knocked him off the ladder onto the cement floor—' She stopped and put a hand to her heart. 'I think it's bad...'

'He's in the barn?' Rafe rapped.

'Mmm.' Liz swallowed. 'Dad's with him...'

'Don't move him.' Rafe was firm. 'I'll get my bag.'

'Oh, Lizzie, I'm so sorry.' Toni grabbed her friend's arm. 'Let's get back to Tom.'

'I think he's broken something, Tone.' Liz's composure began slipping. 'Oh, God, we all love him to bits...but the silly old coot climbing ladders at his age—'

'Take it easy, Liz,' Toni counselled. 'You have to think like a nurse here and not as Tom's granddaughter. For starters, we'll need some blankets and a pillow. And what about Tom's medical history? Do you know if he's taking any medication?'

'Oh, God, I don't...' Liz's voice cracked and she clamped her lips hard, struggling with her tumbled emotions.

'You're around Tom a lot, Lizzie. For heaven's sake, think!'

'Sorry—I don't know.' Liz's mouth wobbled.

'Well, do you know who his GP is?'

'Reid McAndrew. Tom's been his patient for years.'

'Then get on to him and see what you can find out,' Toni said urgently.

Liz shook her head. 'It's Saturday—he could be anywhere!'

'He'll have an answering service. They'll tell you where to find him. And if all else fails, ring his wife. She's listed under her business name, Andrea Charles. Can you remember that?'

Liz repeated the name. 'But if I can't get onto anyone, Rafe will know what to do, won't he?' she asked desperately.

'It will be a lot easier if he has some history. But he'll do his best for Tom, you know that. Have you rung for an ambulance?'

'Mmm—Mum was doing that. Dad's a mess...'

Toni bit her lips together, dragging her professionalism up from her toes. She had to be doubly strong for Liz, who seemed to have lost it completely. 'Now, you go for the blankets and make the phone calls and I'll go to Tom.' They were at the barn door. 'Rafe will find us. He won't be far behind.'

Rafe was running as though his life depended on it. Worst-case scenario could be a severe break. The resultant blood loss could prove fatal, especially to someone of Tom's advanced age. He hoped not. For all their sakes.

It was definitely a fractured neck of femur. Toni saw at once the irregularity of Tom's right leg. It was fractionally shorter than the other and sitting painfully out of joint. She looked up thankfully as Rafe burst in through the barn door and joined her at Tom's side.

'Silly old buzzard...' Cliff Marchant kept repeating. 'I'd have got the damned pony feed for him but, no, he's got to be independent...'

'Cliff, I know you're upset,' Rafe said firmly, 'but railing against your dad won't help. Now...' he turned to Toni '...what do we know?'

Toni relayed what had been set in train. 'And I've checked his pulse. It's weak and thready. His oxygen sats would have to be low as well.'

'We can't do much about that until the ambulance gets here,' Rafe said. 'Just let's hope we have a bit more joy about Tom's history when Liz gets back.'

Tom began muttering incoherently, his restive movements alerting Rafe.

'It's OK, Tom. You've had a fall, mate. We're getting help for you.'

Gently, Toni brushed the fine silver hair back from the elderly man's forehead. 'Will you give him some pain relief?'

'I'll give him a jab of morphine.' Rafe shot open his case. 'Plus Maxolon to combat any nausea. But I'd be a lot happier if I knew some history.'

'Oh—' Toni shot up from her kneeling position. 'Here's Lizzie now!'

Liz took a moment to get her breath. 'I got Dr McAndrew on his mobile. He…said he's prescribed digoxin for Tom.'

The medication was used to strengthen the action of the heart. Rafe's gaze narrowed in conjecture. With that kind of history perhaps the elderly man had become giddy. It would explain his fall. 'Right. At least that gives us something to go on. Well done, Liz.'

Liz dropped to her grandfather's side and took his hand. 'He's never said anything about his health. We all thought he was as fit as. But he's not…' Her voice cracked.

'Lizzie, I need your help here,' Toni said bracingly. 'Let's make use of these blankets and get Tom more comfortable.'

'I can do that.' Liz seemed grateful to be doing something.

'And, Cliff, might be an idea if you'd keep a look out for the ambulance,' Rafe said. 'Direct them over here to the barn, OK?'

'Uh—yes.' Cliff scrambled upright. 'I'll tell them to back up as close as they can.' He looked at his daughter. 'What's your mum doing, love?'

'She's phoning the boys to let them know. And she'll pack a bag for Granddad for hospital.' Liz took a steadying breath. 'Dad, he'll be all right. Rafe's here and he's a fine doctor. We couldn't have anyone better to look after Granddad.'

'Yeah. Thanks, Doc...' Cliff seemed to pull himself together and then began making his way outside.

Within seconds of the ambulance's arrival Rafe began issuing orders. 'Let's get our patient on oxygen. Antonia, will you monitor Tom, please?' He turned to the paramedic. 'Mr Marchant needs fluids, mate. We'll run Haemaccel, stat.'

'Right you are, Doc. I'll hook up the heart monitor as well.'

'Excellent, thanks.' Rafe's hands moved skilfully to secure a line to receive the IV fluids. 'How're the oxygen sats, Toni?'

'Low. Eighty-nine per cent.'

Rafe scrubbed a hand across his cheekbones. He wasn't surprised. But he was placing his bets on the heart monitor telling him more. Seconds later his prognosis was confirmed. Tom was showing every sign of being in atrial fibrillation. And although that didn't mean his condition was life-threatening, he was certainly very ill.

He'd make a more in-depth investigation when they'd got Tom to Resus. If a digoxin boost was indicated, it could be introduced very carefully through an IV. He sent a swift look towards Liz. 'Mobile reception OK from here? I need to get onto the hospital.'

'Should be.' Liz bit her lip. 'He'll need surgery, won't he?'

'I'm afraid he will, Liz,' Rafe said gently. 'But Tom's a tough cookie...' Rafe left the sentence unfinished, stepping away he hit a number on speed dial. 'Amy? Rafe. I'm bringing in Tom Marchant. Probable NOF repair. Could you alert Keith, please?'

'There we might have a problem.' Amy was calm. 'Keith's already in Theatre. Young biker came off at speed with resultant pelvic injury.'

'OK...' Rafe expelled a hard breath. 'Do we have enough staff available to assist in Theatre Two?'

'On call as needed,' Amy said. 'And Grace is available to gas.'

'Excellent. I'll scrub, then. I'll need all orthorpaedic trays sterilised and ready, please, Amy. Could you organise all that, asap?'

'I'll get onto it now.'

'Thanks. Our ETA is around thirty minutes.' Rafe closed off his mobile to find Toni standing silently by his side.

'Are you sure about this?' she asked quietly.

'I'm accredited to perform surgery, Antonia.'

'I'm not questioning your ability.' Her eyes clouded. 'It's just...'

His jaw tightened. 'You're doubting my physical stamina?'

'You've been through a lot recently—' She stopped and clamped her lips together.

'I wouldn't do this if I thought I'd be compromising Tom's outcome. This is *my* decision, Antonia.'

In other words, butt out. Toni gave the semblance of a nod. 'Will you travel with Tom?'

'Yes. And they're about ready for me. Sorry to do this to you again.' He tossed her his keys. 'Could you drive my car back to town, please? Just leave it in the doctors' car park and the keys at the nurses' station. I'll pick them up when I'm through. And, Toni?'

She tilted her chin at him. 'Yes?'

'I'll be a while. *Don't hang about.*'

Of course she'd hang about. Toni's fingers tightened on

his keys. She'd want to be there for Liz and her family. As for anything else? Well, that was her business.

It was almost eight o'clock that evening. Toni sat with Liz in the staffroom. Liz had shooed her parents off and they'd gone to get a bite to eat. She looked bleakly into her third cup of coffee. 'Life can change in a minute, can't it?'

Toni huffed dryly. 'Make that a second. One or two words can change a life for ever.' Words like *I'm married. You have cancer. The baby's not viable.*

Oh, good grief. Toni suppressed a shiver. I'm getting morbid. She rose to her feet. 'Another coffee?'

'God, no. I'm all coffeed out.' Liz sighed. 'How much longer?'

Toni glanced at her watch. 'We should hear any time now.'

No sooner had she'd spoken than Rafe pushed through the louvred doors into the staffroom. Toni felt her stomach twist at his grave demeanour. Had something gone wrong with Tom's surgery?

'How is he, Rafe?' Liz was on her feet. 'I asked Theatre to ring here when—'

'I decided to let you know myself,' Rafe broke in.

'And?'

Rafe finally smiled. 'Everything went well, Liz. Tom's in Recovery.'

'Oh…' Liz's voice cracked. 'Thank you so much, Rafe. Thank you…'

Rafe lifted a blocking hand. 'You should be able to see your granddad in a half-hour or so.'

'That'll just give me time to collect Mum and Dad from the coffee shop.' Liz was already gathering up her bag. She sprinted for the door and then turned back. 'Toni…thanks for…well, you know…'

Toni waggled a finger wave. 'You're welcome, Lizzie. Take care.' She stood, and sent a level glance at Rafe. 'Cup of tea? Won't take a minute.'

Rafe shook his head. 'Why are you still here, Antonia?'

Seeing his closed expression, Toni felt wrong-footed. 'I'm here for Liz and her parents.'

'It's been hours. They wouldn't have expected that. And I'd specifically asked you not to hang about.'

'*Ordered*, more like,' she countered sharply. 'What's your problem, Rafe?'

'I don't have one,' he said grittily. 'But apparently you do. With me.'

'With you?' Toni's voice rose interrogatively. 'What do you mean, *with you*?'

'I don't need a minder, Antonia.'

Toni's heartbeat surged to a sickening rhythm. Was that what he thought she was doing there? 'Get over yourself, Rafe.'

His brows twitched into a frown. 'What's that supposed to mean?'

'I didn't *need* to be here,' she said. 'But I stayed. For Liz, of course, but mostly for you. I foolishly thought you might have appreciated a bit of professional support after the op, a bit of down time to just…talk.'

Rafe stared at her in silence for a moment, his jaw clenched. 'In other words, you were keeping a watching brief on my professionalism. Maybe you even had me breaking down in the middle of surgery so you could say, *I told you so*?'

'Nothing was further from my mind.' Two spots of colour glazed Toni's cheeks. 'I don't know what kinds of problems are still bugging you, Rafe but don't presume to disrespect my reasons for being here. Don't disrespect *me*.'

In one fluid movement she threw his keys on to the

table, her breath coming hard and fast. 'You're not the man I thought you were!' Hauling her shoulder bag off the back of the chair, she gave him one last disdainful glare and stormed out.

'Antonia! Toni, wait…!'

Toni's response to Rafe's urgent plea was to walk even faster until she was out of the building. Her thoughts were in turmoil. How could he have misjudged her actions so badly? She'd wanted to wait with Liz. That's what friends did. And if that meant she was around for Rafe as well, that wasn't a crime, was it? But he'd gone and accused her of having a hidden agenda. And instead of feeling supported by her presence, he'd interpreted her motives as those of almost spying on him.

Did he feel vulnerable because of what he'd confided to her about his past? Both professionally and personally?

Whatever, it was clear he didn't trust her as a colleague, a friend, and as for anything deeper—forget it.

Anger and pain fought for equal room in her heart. Words again. Words said in anger. Words that could injure a heart, kill a hope.

Destroy a budding love affair.

Her throat tightened as she made her way along the street to the taxi rank and climbed into the first waiting cab.

'Where to, love?' the cabbie asked.

Bleakly Toni gave him her address. Sinking back into the cushioned seat, she thanked heaven for the safety of home.

Rafe felt like ramming his fist through the wall. Had he learned nothing from the past? It seemed he couldn't even differentiate between the amazing level of trust that Antonia had offered and the two-faced version from

Gabrielle. Antonia was worth a hundred of her. A thousand! She'd done nothing, other than offer her support, listened to the story of his heartbreak, trusted him with her own. And he'd lashed her to pieces with his rant.

Was he so afraid of getting close to a woman again that he'd struck out the way he had? Get her before she got him? Was that it? He shook his head. He was like a fighter who couldn't let down his guard for fear of being hurt. Well, now he'd been the one doing the hurting. He'd hurt Antonia irrevocably. She was gone.

Moving across to the window, he reached out like a blind man towards the sill, gripping it with both hands, staring out at the night. God, whoever said *sorry* was the hardest word had had it right. But somehow he'd have to find a way to say it.

But whether or not she'd listen was another matter entirely.

Well, another one bites the dust, Toni thought bitterly as she opened her front door and went inside. She stopped and looked around her. It seemed an eternity since she'd been here with Rafe this morning. This morning when everything between them had seemed so promising, so wonderfully new and…safe. For the first time in a long time she'd begun to trust again. Now everything was ashes.

Something in her heart scrunched tight. It hurt so much that he didn't trust her. More than hurt. It felt as though he'd cut out her heart and left nothing behind.

Despondently, she stripped off her clothes and stepped under the shower, telling herself she was a survivor. She'd damned well better be. Dressed in a pair of silk sleep shorts and a vest top, she felt marginally better. Going to the kitchen, she peered into the fridge but found nothing to

interest her. The freezer was a better option and she took
out a tub of chocolate-chip ice cream.

A few spoonfuls of ice cream later she sighed and replaced the tub in the freezer. Perhaps she'd make some
peppermint tea but, then, perhaps she wouldn't.

When her doorbell rang, she stood stock still, her heart
going into freefall. If that was Rafe—and it would be—
she couldn't deal with him now. Just go away, she pleaded
silently. But it seemed her caller wasn't going anywhere.

Her hands trembled slightly as she smoothed them down
the sides of her shorts. She was hardly dressed for company but he'd seen her in a bikini so what she was wearing was modest by comparison. 'OK, OK,' she muttered,
heading off along the hallway to the front door. She swung
the door open and they stood there looking at one another.

Toni felt goose-bumps break out all over her, felt the
atmosphere between them tightening like the strings of a
violin. He'd obviously been home and changed. His hair
was ruffled, still damp from the shower. And she was so
pleased to see him it almost hurt. Lifting her chin, she
said with as much coolness as she could manage, 'Are
you going to stand there glaring at me or would you like
to come in?'

For a second Rafe's wintergreen gaze seem to lose its
colour, glaze over and go still. Giving an almost imper-
ceptible inclination of his head, he said, 'I'd like to come
in, if it's all right…?'

Toni stood aside, allowed him through, and then closed
the door behind him. She led the way to the lounge. And
then turned and faced him.

Rafe felt his heart spin out of rhythm. Yet her response
was more, much more forgiving than he'd expected, indeed deserved. He shifted from one foot to the other, his
hands jammed into the back pockets of his cargos. 'I'd like

to apologise for my appalling behaviour earlier. I've hurt you and I'm deeply sorry.'

'And so you should be...' Toni's teeth caught her bottom lip. 'I...thought we'd come such a long way, Rafe. In every way that counted...'

He was silent for a long moment and then he let his breath out in a ragged sigh. 'And then I dismantled everything in a few seconds flat.'

'You have issues with trust and I can understand that after what happened with your ex-wife. But I'm not *her*, Rafe. I never will be. You have to let me in.' Toni paused, swallowing back the well of emotion that rose in her chest. 'That's if you want to...'

'Oh, God, yes.' Rafe allowed himself no more time to ponder, to hesitate, to start weighing up the pros and cons. Everything he wanted, needed was here. With this woman. This woman of the generous spirit, the forgiving heart. The lover he wanted for his own.

'Oh, Rafe...' Toni took a deep-throated swallow as he reached out and gathered her in.

'Don't say anything,' he murmured. 'Just let me hold you.'

Toni wasn't sure when the wordless comfort changed or even if it did. Perhaps it just grew and took on a life of its own, drawing them into one volatile storm of emotions.

She shivered when Rafe's hands began to smooth her back and shoulders, moving until his fingers were bracketing her head and his hands were holding her with infinite gentleness, while he kissed her with deep tenderness, deep giving.

Making a little sound in her throat, she curled against him and when his kiss deepened she welcomed it, oh, how she welcomed it, opening her mouth to his, wanting it all.

Suddenly, out of nowhere, she felt an enormous sense

of freedom, a sense of rightness she'd never felt before. And when his ragged declaration came, *'You're everything I want,'* she felt so physical, so alive.

Rafe felt the shudder that ran through her as she arched up against him with a little cry. He told himself to take it slowly but that was never going to be the way of it. The soft waistband of her shorts came away to allow him the access he craved. With the utmost care for her, he traced the bowl of her pelvis and lower... 'Let's not do this here, Toni,' he breathed hoarsely. 'Come to bed with me—if that's what you want too?'

'Yes.' One word. That's all it needed for Rafe to lift her right off her feet in celebration and then to gently lower her until her feet touched the floor again. Then, slowly and deliberately, stopping to kiss along the way, they finally made it to the bedroom.

Their lovemaking was slow, dreamlike, hushed sounds of delight, of ecstasy as they pleasured one another. Then there was no going back. And all of it—everything else in the entire world—became meaningless against the flood tide of their shared release.

They slept for a while and then made love again and around midnight they had a crazy, fun-filled shower together. After that they raided Toni's fridge and cooked eggs and bacon and drank big mugs of tea.

And talked.

'In my whole life I've never been so happy,' Toni said.

Rafe leaned across and took her hand, running his thumb along the tips of her fingers. 'You make me feel brand new.'

She smiled indulgently. 'That's the name of a song.'

'Is it?' His mouth turned down comically. 'I thought I was being original.'

His look changed and became serious. 'I still can't believe how forgiving you've been, Antonia.'

'Why?' She lifted a shoulder dismissively. 'I'm a fairly straightforward kind of person. If things are muddled, I like to deal with them—not let them fester. And we've sorted things now, haven't we?'

He sent her a guarded smile. 'I guess we have.' He should tell her about the PTSD but now wasn't the time. He'd get round to it. She'd probably guessed most of it anyway.

'Mind you, if you hadn't come round tonight, I might have given you a wide berth at work next week.'

'I would have hated that,' he said honestly.

'Mmm, me too.' Toni blocked a yawn. 'So, are we going back to bed?'

'Ah…' Rafe sought for an excuse that sounded plausible. But he couldn't risk the possibility of the nightmares recurring and frightening the daylights out of her. He hadn't had one for a while now, but if they were going to happen, they usually happened in the early hours. He needed to be gone. 'I'll take off, I think. Bit to think about.'

'I see…' Although clearly she didn't. 'But you're OK with us—aren't you?'

'Oh, yes! Don't ever doubt that. I want to be up early as well, check in on Tom.'

Toni sent him one of her bewitching smiles. 'And if you stayed, there's a possibility—just a slight one—you might be *delayed?*'

'More a probability.' Rafe jumped at the flimsy excuse.

Their farewell was long and tender. 'Will I see you tomorrow—I mean today?' Toni asked as they stood achingly close to each other.

'Have a sleep in,' Rafe urged, 'and then come round to me for a swim. I'll dazzle you with something for lunch.'

She gave a throaty chuckle. 'Something from the deli, I'll bet.'

'It's a great deli,' he protested. 'And I'll be selective.' He pressed his forehead to hers. 'Everything about this seems right, doesn't it?'

'Oh, yes...' Toni was dazzled with the newness of it.

Instead of taking his leave, Rafe held her more tightly, amazed at the way their bodies called to one another, how every dip and curve in her willowy suppleness found a home in his.

'Go now,' she whispered, and gave him a little push towards the door. 'You need your sleep too.'

He reached out a finger, his touch feather-like along her jaw, her throat into the soft hollow of her collarbone. 'I think this is boots and all for me, Antonia.'

'Me too,' she whispered, her voice hardly there.

CHAPTER NINE

Monday morning.

TONI came in to work early but it seemed Liz had beaten her to it. They were the only ones in the staffroom. 'Well, isn't this a treat?' Toni smiled, dropping her bag and taking a mug from the dishwasher. 'Having the place to ourselves for two minutes, I mean.'

'Mmm,' Liz said automatically, mug of coffee at her side, her chin resting on her upturned hand.

'Gorgeous morning outside.' Toni gave a theatrical sigh. 'Just the kind of day to take off and play hooky.'

Liz's head shot up. That didn't sound like their conscientious nurse manager. 'Well, well.' Her eyes opened to questioning wideness. 'Who's looking all chirpy and loved up this morning? What *did* you get up to on the weekend, Ms Morell?'

Toni gave a Mona Lisa smile, for once not responding to her friend's mild teasing. Picking up her coffee, she sat opposite Liz at the table. 'How's Tom?'

'I've just popped up to see him. Poor old love…' Liz stopped, her voice becoming husky. 'He looks a bit fragile, actually.'

'Still confused from the effect of the anaesthetic, probably,' Toni commiserated. 'But that'll reverse in a day or so, Lizzy.'

'Yes, I know all that but it's awful seeing someone so vital as Granddad…cut down.'

Toni gave a tut. 'Lizzy, he'll recover quite quickly, according to Rafe. He's very pleased with him. In fact, he's hoping to have Tom up in a day or two and beginning some physio on a rollator.'

'That soon!' Liz brightened. 'Then Rafe must be very confident about Tom's recovery. He's going to need several weeks' rehab, though, isn't he?'

'Of course. That's standard.'

'I doubt Dad will want him living on his own again.'

'Well, plenty of time to think about that,' Toni said. 'Just be glad Tom is still with us.'

'Thanks to Rafe.' Liz's hands spanned her mug. 'Did you both have a nice day at the farm on Saturday?'

And later. Toni gave an inward smile. That information was not for sharing. 'Yes, it was wonderful. Have you got everything squared away at Blue Hills?'

'Mostly.' Liz rocked a hand. 'Dad and the boys will take it in turns to go out each day and check on the animals. Other than that, we just have to keep Tom happy and get him on his feet again.'

'That's the way,' Toni said bracingly. 'Let me know if I can do anything.' She stood, taking her coffee. 'That sounds like the fairy footsteps of the team so I'll take handover and then I have to consult with Rafe about a couple of things. Are you up to allocating jobs or would you rather have a quiet day?'

'I'm fine.' Liz flapped a hand. 'I'd rather keep busy.' Her mouth pleated at the corners. 'Go and have your tryst. Oops!' Liz gave an exaggerated pout and placed the tips of her fingers over her lips.

Toni flashed her a wry grin. 'Early days, Lizzy.'

'Of course.' Liz nodded. 'I think it's lovely, by the way.'

Rafe couldn't believe how energised he felt, especially for a Monday morning. And he couldn't stop grinning like an idiot. Heck, he felt like a teenager in love for the first time. That thought brought him up short. As did the swift knock on his door.

'Oh…' Toni popped her head in. 'I wondered if you were in.'

'As you see.' He held out his arms and she ran straight into them. 'Good morning…' His smile was tender.

Toni's mouth curved. 'Good *night* as well. You OK?'

'Better than OK.'

Their kiss started gently but in a second they were on fire for each other. Rafe growled deep in his throat and lifted his head. 'That's what I call beginning the day on a high. You smell like roses.'

'Do I?' She cupped his face with both hands. 'And you smell like summer.'

He grimaced. 'Not sweaty summer?'

'No.' She laughed softly. 'Nice summer. Soap and water summer.'

Rafe stepped back, parking himself on the edge of his desk and folding his arms. 'Actually, I was about to come and find you. I wanted to pass on some good news. Bernie Maguire called me. The Rotary club has purchased acreage a little way out of town. They're calling tenders to build a retirement village. The plans he outlined sound just what our seniors need and it will include a nursing facility for those who need a bit of extra care.'

'Oh, that's amazing!' Toni pressed her hands together under her chin. 'Is it going to be self-contained units?'

'More like one-bedroomed cottages, from what Bernie

said. They're hoping some of the seniors will want to do a bit of gardening, keep a small pet if they'd like to.'

'So, folk like Denis will have somewhere nice to live and be as independent as they want to be.'

Rafe grinned. 'Bernie's pretending he thought of the idea himself, of course. But if it gets the job done…'

'Well done, you.'

'And you,' he insisted. 'You inspire me, Antonia. You really do.'

Toni blushed. 'Perhaps we inspire each other. Now, I have a casualty department to run, Doctor…'

He slid off the desk. 'Now *I* need a hug before you go.'

Four weeks later, Tom Marchant was released from hospital.

Rafe, Toni and Liz watched as Liz's parents shepherded Tom into their car. He was going to stay with them for the time being.

'Granddad would far rather be going home to Blue Hills,' Liz lamented.

'I'm sure he would.' Rafe was sympathetic. 'But even you can see he can't be on his own at the moment, Liz.'

'But later on, in the future?' She looked hopefully at the registrar.

Rafe lifted a shoulder. 'If he keeps up his physio and his general health remains good, he'll possibly be able to go back.'

'Come on, Lizzy,' Toni cajoled. 'Tom is gutsy. He'll dig in and do whatever it takes to get back into life.'

Liz looked wry. 'I'm being a pain, whereas you two have been so good to Tom while he's been in.'

Rafe snorted. 'A few games of chess hardly took up much of my time. And Tom is great company. Knows a lot too.' He looked at his watch. 'Now, if you ladies will excuse me, I have an informal meeting with the board. Dig me out if you need to.'

'So, how is it going with you and Rafe?' Liz asked as they walked back to the station.

'Things are fine.' Toni didn't mention that so far they'd not spent an entire night together. Obviously Rafe had his reasons for not staying and she hadn't pushed him.

'Fine?' Liz sent her a puzzled look. 'That seems seriously underwhelming, if I may say so. Are you sure everything's OK?'

Toni's nerves tightened. She would love to have her friend's down-to-earth opinion but there was no way she could share that kind of intimate information. Instead, she gave a warning little eye roll. 'Lizzie...'

'OK.' Liz lifted her hands in retraction. 'I'll mind my own. Just have to keep reminding myself you're all grown up. And you're a savvy chick as well.'

Toni chuckled. 'When were we ever *chicks?*'

'Dunno,' Liz responded blithely. 'But we must have been. Once.'

It was almost at the end of the shift when Rafe stuck his head round the cubicle curtain. 'Antonia, can you get someone else to finish up in here? MVA out on North Road. Ambulance has gone out but they need a doctor at the scene. I'd like you along as well, please.'

'Give me a minute.' Toni apologised to her patient and assigned Amy to take over. Hurrying to the staffroom, she collected a couple of high-visibility vests, designating 'Doctor' and 'Nurse' on the backs, and ran to find Rafe.

He was taking delivery of a trauma kit from Liz, and looked up as Toni joined them at the station. 'All set?'

She nodded. 'Liz, would you hand over, please? Don't know when we'll be back.'

'Absolutely.' Liz waved them away. 'Mind how you go.'

'What do we know?' Toni asked the inevitable question as they headed out of town.

'Two vehicles involved. A fully loaded refrigerated truck coming into town sideswiped a Land Rover going in the opposite direction. Driver of the truck dead at the wheel.' Rafe's jaw clenched and unclenched. 'The weight of the truck has forced the car off the road and it's run downhill and crashed into a belt of scrub.'

'Oh, my lord…' Toni whispered. 'Who's in the car, do we know?'

'Family.'

'So, possibly children?'

Rafe didn't answer.

All emergency services were in attendance when they got to the accident scene. Erin hurried to meet them. 'Not a mark on the truck driver,' she said grimly. 'Possible heart attack. Fortunately, his truck hit an embankment and stopped, otherwise who knows what other damage could have been caused?'

'Who's in the car?' Rafe snapped, pulling on his vest.

'Family. Not sure of the dynamics yet. It seems all the doors on the Land Rover are jammed from the impact. Just lucky it didn't roll. The fire lads have to cut the scrub back from the car first so we can get to them.' Even as Erin spoke, the ripping sound of chainsaws could be heard echoing up from the valley below. 'Stuart and Chris are standing by there,' she said, referring to the other two senior paramedics. 'Brandon is staying with the fatality until the police sort things.'

'Right,' Rafe said tersely. 'Let's get down there, Toni.' He turned to Erin. 'Could you bring both ambulances as close as you can, please? Sounds like we're going to need all the help we can get.'

'And be extra-careful, Erin,' Toni warned. 'That hill is very steep.'

'We've managed to make enough room to get the back doors marginally open, Doc,' Stuart said as Rafe and Toni reached the crashed small car. 'Mum and Dad are in the front and two little kids in the back. Dad's out of it but seems unhurt elsewhere. Mum's trapped and drifting a bit.' He lowered his voice. 'Frantic about the kids in the back. We can't get the door open properly to make any assessment. We need someone small to get in there.'

'I'll go,' Toni said sharply. Already she could hear the pitiful little keening sounds of distress coming from the back seat. Ducking her head, she began to wiggle her way through the half-open door and crawl inside.

'We have to do better than this!' Rafe spoke to one of the firemen. 'I need to get in there, mate. Get the damned doors off!'

'Fair go, Doc.' The fireman said stoically. 'We're doing our best.'

Rafe swore impatiently. 'Toni, what's happening?'

'Two little boys,' Toni reported. As she spoke, her hands were running over one of them, checking his body. 'First one seems OK. I'm checking the other one now.' What she observed sent Toni's clinical instincts into overdrive. The child's chest was heaving but his breath sounds were laboured. Too laboured. They had a problem here. A big one. 'We need to treat this child, Rafe—fast!'

'Right, back doors are off!' The firemen lurched under the heavy weight and dragged the crushed metal out of the way.

Rafe wasted no time. Bending his head, he edged inside the car.

'It's a throat injury,' Toni said urgently. 'He was holding a toy aeroplane. See, the tip of the wing's caught him. It's still in his seat belt.'

'Let's take a look.' Rafe peered down at the injured little boy. 'He's cyanosed. Throat's swelling.'

'And his resps are high,' Toni said. 'Can we move him?'

'No time.' Rafe let his breath go in a stream. He'd have to act fast and intubate immediately to protect the child's airway, otherwise he'd be faced with having to perform a laryngotomy. And the circumstances were far from ideal for that. He stuck his head back out of the door. 'Can someone get the uninjured child out, please? And I need the trauma kit. Now!'

'Please, help my little boy...' The mother's plea came brokenly from the front seat.

For a second Rafe's face contorted and then he seemed to gather himself. 'I'm going to need you to help me here, Toni.'

'I understand. Tell me what you want.'

Rafe's mouth tightened. What he wanted was a sterile theatre and time on his side. And leg room.

Behind them there was a flurry of activity and the trauma kit was shoved onto the now vacant space on the back seat.

Rafe began unzipping sections, gathering equipment. 'Give this little guy hundred per cent oxygen, please, Toni, while I set up.'

Toni quickly had everything in position, holding the mask over the boy's face, giving him every breath of oxygen he could take, the steady rhythmic hiss of the bag drowned out by the din of the cutting tools working to free the parents in the front.

'More oxygen. He's still too light,' Rafe said. 'No way he'll tolerate a tube. That's better. Can you apply some cricoid pressure, please.'

Toni automatically complied. Using her thumb, she squeezed pressure on the cricoid cartilage. The action would stop any possibility of reflux from the child's stomach into his airway. 'Airway secured,' she reported quietly.

With quick precision, Rafe found a vein, inserted the cannula and injected the anaesthetic, just enough to knock his small patient out so he could be intubated without further distress.

The muscle relaxant took effect almost instantaneously. 'He's out,' Toni said.

'OK...gentle manoeuvre here,' Rafe murmured. Without moving the child's neck, he simply lifted his jaw forward, slipping the laryngoscope into his mouth and then sliding the tube in. 'Cricoid pressure off,' he directed, quickly attaching the tube to the oxygen supply. Snatching up the stethoscope, he listened to the little boy's lungs for breath sounds as he bagged him.

'He's looking better already.' Toni's voice was hushed in relief.

Rafe nodded. 'I want him on a spinal board and out of here. Erin, will you go with him?' He turned to the paramedic, who was leaning over from the front seat, the parents having been removed. 'He'll need careful monitoring.'

'I'll watch him every second.' Erin looked slightly in awe. 'That's some skill you have there, Doctor. You just saved that child's life.'

Rafe grunted a non-reply. 'Over to you,' he said instead. 'I'll look at the parents now.'

Toni stood closely beside Rafe as they watched the second ambulance take off slowly up the hill to the road. Suddenly Rafe turned his back on the sight and sank to the ground, his head drooping almost to his knees.

'Rafe?' Immediately, Toni dropped beside him. She

touched his shoulders, finding them taut and stiff. 'Are you OK?'

He brought his head up and looked at her bleakly. 'Why do we do this job?'

Toni shrugged. 'Are we deranged, do you think?'

He gave a hollow laugh. 'It's quite possible. You were brilliant, Toni.'

'Just part of the team,' she said modestly.

'You should really think about becoming a doctor.'

She made a face. 'I like doing what I do. I'll leave the heavy lifting to clever chaps like you.'

He rolled back his shoulders and lay on the grass, putting out a hand and tugging her down beside him.

'Thank goodness that little family will be all right.' Toni smiled at him as his arm went under her head and she tucked in beside him. The father had suffered concussion but otherwise seemed unhurt, and although the children's mother had some deep cuts and was obviously very shocked, she too would recover well. 'They'll keep the whole family in, won't they?'

'Keith will sort them. Did we get the names of the boys?'

'Nicholas and Harry. Harry caused the drama.'

'Young Harry, hmm?' Rafe turned his head and kissed her gently. 'Coming home with me?'

At last. Toni's chest lifted in a long sigh. 'Yes, please.'

It was the early hours when Rafe woke. Toni's rhythmic breathing, the fluttering of her lashes on her cheek told him she was sound asleep. Her hair in all its silken glory rippled over the pillow. He knew if he bent and kissed her, her skin would be baby-soft and warm. He watched almost spellbound as she turned over and curled up, resisting the urge to run the tip of his finger along the fine-boned outline of her spine. Instead, he got quietly out of bed and padded to the window to look out over the garden and the soft beginning of a brand-new day.

But it was still too early to be up and he didn't want to wake her. Slipping back under the sheet, he closed his eyes. He needn't have worried after all. His sleep had been undisturbed.

Rafe's harsh cry woke Toni with a start.

She jerked upright, her heart pounding. 'Rafe...' Her hand went to his shoulder. He was tangled in the bed-clothes, between sleep and wakefulness and caught in the grip of some awful nightmare. His muffled pleas of desperation tore at Toni's heart. 'Rafe, wake up,' she urged softly. 'It's OK... It's OK... Hush...'

His moan became a shuddering breath. 'It's all right.' Toni bent over him, cradling his dark head against her, murmuring reassurances over and over. Finally, he went still and she sensed he'd woken fully but it was a long time until he moved. His eyes flicked open and he looked at her. 'So now you know,' he said bitterly.

Toni's arms tightened around him as it all fell into place—the reasons why he never stayed the entire night with her. The nightmares were obviously a symptom of post-traumatic stress. And he'd been trying to hide it from her.

She looked down at him. He'd covered his eyes with his forearm. 'Do you want to talk?'

He shook his head. 'Not now,' he said tersely.

'Then when, Rafe?' Toni was determined not to let this go.

For answer, he shook his head and said nothing.

Toni felt suddenly alienated. This was hardly adult be-haviour from him and she deserved better. *They* deserved better. She made a snap decision. 'I'll go home, then. I need to shower and get ready for work.'

'You could do that here.'

No, she couldn't. Couldn't pretend things were normal when he obviously still had a load of baggage to deal with. *Baggage* he refused to share with her.

'I think it's best if I go. You obviously need your space.'

'Sorry.' He removed his forearm and spun to face her, an almost feverish sheen in his eyes.

A tiny frown lingered for a second on her forehead. 'For what?'

He worked his fingers across his eyes. 'This debacle...'

'It's not your fault, Rafe.' And if he couldn't get past that, how were they to go on? She slid out of bed. 'I'll... see you at work later.'

Toni arrived at work with her mind spinning, her thoughts so tangled, it felt like they'd run into a brick wall and bounced back to engulf her. She had to talk to Rafe. Correction, *he* had to open up and talk to her. He hadn't managed to do it up to now and time was running out for that to happen. In only a matter of weeks his tenure here would be over.

She had a management meeting first thing and, leaving Liz to take handover, Toni took herself off to the second floor, where the nurse managers were scheduled to meet. She greeted her contemporaries and, grabbing a coffee, took her place in the circle.

Larissa Grant, the DON, looked around the group and said, 'We're all busy people, so if no one has any urgent business, we'll keep today's meeting short.'

There were murmurs of relief and the meeting wound up in record time. Toni sped back to Casualty.

'Thank goodness you're back,' Liz said. 'All hell's broken loose in here.'

'What do we have, Lizzie?'

The senior nurse grimaced. 'The high-school bus ran off the road and hit a tree. Fortunately, the driver had only begun his pick-up from the outlying farms so there weren't many kids on board.'

'Usual driver?'

''Mmm. Gordon Aspinall. He's very reliable so it could be a problem with the bus.'

'Well, that's for the police,' Toni dismissed. 'What casualties do we have?'

'Well, Gordon himself, who needs to be checked over, and two students. One sixteen-year-old female with a knee injury and the other is a fourteen-year-old, Damon Spiteri. He hit his forehead on the metal bar of the seat in front of him. Justin is presently suturing him. He was pretty bloody and a bit shocked so Justin took him first.'

'OK...' Toni blew out a resigned breath. She hadn't needed another road accident coming on top of yesterday's. But, then, neither did the victims. 'Is Rafe in, do you know?'

'Just arrived, I think. I'll page him.'

'Thanks. Meanwhile, I'll pop my head in on the girl. Do we have her name?'

'Kristal Holmes. And you'll need all your PR skills. Her mother's just arrived and is on the warpath. Apparently, Kristal was due to audition for some cheerleading dance thing. I reckon nothing less than Gordon being sent to jail will convince Mrs Holmes we're doing our job.'

'Oh, bliss,' Toni sighed. 'Nothing like being the meat in the sandwich. I'll see if I can sort things.'

Liz gave a wry smile. 'You're good at that.'

Except where it counted most. Toni walked quickly towards the cubicles. Swishing back the curtain, she could see at a glance it was going to be one of *those* encounters. 'Mrs Holmes?' she queried the thin blonde woman who was hovering impatiently.

'Yes. And about time my daughter was looked at.'

Toni turned to the teenager on the treatment couch. 'Hi, Kristal. I'm Toni. Can you tell me where you're hurt?'

'It's my knee.' Blocking a tear with the tips of her fingers, the youngster tried to sit up.

'Stay there, honey.' Toni squeezed her shoulder. 'The doctor will be with you shortly.'

'That Gordon Aspinall should be jailed for what he's done.' The mother's tone was bordering on warlike. 'Kristal was selected to audition for the cheerleading squad for one of the big Sydney football teams next week. She's got an agent and everything—and now look at her...'

All heads turned as one as the curtains swished back and Rafe strode in. Judging by his tight-lipped expression, Toni guessed Liz had already briefed him. 'This is Dr Riccardi,' she jumped in diplomatically. 'Doctor, this is Mrs Holmes and her daughter, Kristal, who was brought in as a result of an accident with the school bus this morning.'

Acknowledging Toni's information with a curt nod, Rafe hitched himself against a corner of the treatment couch and asked, 'Where are you hurt, Kristal?'

'She's hurt her knee!' With an exasperated sigh, Mrs Holmes sent her gaze heavenwards. 'How many more times do we have to explain before you do something?'

'Mrs Holmes.' Rafe folded his arms, his lean jaw set as he swivelled to address the woman. 'I'd appreciate it if you'd let Kristal speak for herself, otherwise I may have to ask you to leave.'

'You can't do that!' The mother was clearly outraged. 'My daughter is underage. I have to be here.'

Rafe's jaw tightened. After the soul-destroying start to his morning, his tolerance was on a short fuse. 'Perhaps you'd sit quietly, then, while I examine my patient.'

With a little sniff the mother took a couple of steps back and perched on the edge of a chair Toni held for her.

'Now, Kristal.' Rafe turned to his young patient and asked gently, 'Like to tell me what happened?'

The teenager blinked fast and swallowed. 'I was thrown off the seat when the bus hit the tree. I landed really hard on my right knee. It was all a bit scary but Mr Aspinall looked after us and called our parents and the ambulance and kept us all calm...'

'That's good...' Rafe nodded slowly. He wasn't about to hurry the youngster, since it was essential she debrief in her own time. Poor kid. He guessed she'd not been able to get a word in edgeways since her mother had come on the scene. 'And did you feel the pain right away?'

'Mmm. My knee felt all wobbly.'

'Right. Antonia, if you'd give me a hand, please, we'll get Kristal more comfortable.'

'Just relax, sweetie.' Toni smiled, easing off the girl's trainers. Today she was dressed in her sports strip of shorts and polo shirt so access to her knee was made simple.

'OK, let's see what we have.' Rafe worked the knee slightly and Kristal gasped. His eyes narrowed. 'Would this be an old sports injury, by any chance?'

'I'm not sure. Sometimes it feels...not sore exactly...'

'But a bit uncomfortable?'

Kristal clenched her bottom lip and nodded.

'Has she broken anything?' Mrs Holmes's tone still had an accusing edge.

'No, I'm sure she hasn't,' Rafe responded with studied calm. 'Kristal, you've obviously partly dislocated your patella. Your kneecap. We'll give you some pain relief and pop it back in for you.'

'OK…' The youngster managed a shaky smile.

'So, how is high school going?' Rafe chatted for a minute while the pain relief took effect.

'It's good. I'm captain of the netball team. I take dance lessons as well.'

Rafe listened, making an appropriate comment here and there as he worked her patella gently, ensuring it was relocated. 'There you are. All done. We'll get a support bandage on that for you now. Any problems, come straight back to Casualty. In the meantime, no undue stress on your knee. So, sorry, kiddo, it looks like your audition will have to wait for another time.'

'This is outrageous!' The girl's mother flew to her feet. 'This was Kristal's chance to get into the big time. To be noticed. Maybe get on TV.' She took a step towards Rafe. 'That Gordon Aspinall should be brought to account. He's obviously been drinking and I hope you're going to blood-test him, Doctor. You mark my words, it'll be over the limit. You—'

'Do you have a medical degree, Mrs Holmes?' Rafe cut in, his voice lethally cool.

Her jaw dropped. 'Of course I don't.'

'Well, I do. So I'll be the one to decide what treatment, if any, is appropriate for Mr Aspinall. Is that clear?'

Blotchy patches of red stood out on the woman's cheeks. Suddenly her aggression collapsed like a pack of cards and she burst into tears.

'Mum, don't…' Kristal looked on in distress. 'It's OK.'

'It's not OK…' Mrs Holmes hiccuped a sob. 'I wanted this so much for you, Kristal.'

Enough! Tight-lipped, Rafe walked out.

'Mrs Holmes, sit down again, please.' Toni strove to

restore calm. 'I know how disappointed you must be for Kristal.'

'Yes...'

'Of course you are.' Toni passed the box of tissues to her.

'Thank you, Sister. You've been very kind.' The mother's voice was muffled as she mopped up. 'You never know what's round the corner, do you?'

'No, you certainly don't.' Toni's agreement was heartfelt. 'Back in a tick.' She touched a hand to Mrs Holmes's shoulder and stepped out of the cubicle to find Rafe pacing restlessly.

He stared at her for a long moment, his jaw clenched, before he asked directly, 'Could you delegate someone else to finish up in there, please? I'd like you with me when I examine the bus driver.'

Toni frowned. 'Do you need me as a witness?'

'After that performance in there?' His tone echoed disgust. 'You bet I do.'

Toni called Mel, who was passing, and handed over Kristal's care. Turning back to Rafe, she said tersely, 'Gordon Aspinall is in cube three. And for goodness' sake don't jump all over him.'

'You think I came on too strongly with Mrs Holmes?'

Toni's shoulder lifted in a tight shrug. 'She'd try the patience of a saint but you could have been kinder,' she added, her comment sharp and to the point.

Rafe's mouth pulled tight. Toni's frustration and disappointment with him were palpable. He rubbed at the back of his neck. Dammit. Judging by the way things had gone pear-shaped between them this morning, he'd have done better to have pulled rank and taken himself off for the day. He drew in a long breath and let it go. 'Fill me in a bit, then, would you, please?'

'Gordon is as steady as they come. Well liked in the town. I can't imagine he'd be drinking. And he'd never risk the kids' lives with an unsafe bus.'

'What age group?'

Toni considered. 'Early sixties, possibly.'

Rafe's mouth drew in. This could all be more complicated than anyone thought. Various possibilities for the accident passed through his mind and, unfortunately for Gordon, he couldn't discount any of them.

'I'll just check Mel has everything she needs.' Toni broke into his thoughts abruptly. 'Do you want to go ahead with Gordon and I'll be with you presently?'

'Uh—yes.' He managed a tight smile. 'Thanks for the heads up.'

'You're welcome to my help any time, Rafe. You should know that by now.'

Rafe's jaw clenched and unclenched. He couldn't doubt her sincerity. His heart twisted as he watched his lover hurry away. He wanted, needed to sort things with her but his mind was in overload. Feeling as though a giant steel hand had taken hold of his guts, he forced his mind into neutral and went in search of his patient.

Pulling back the curtains on cubicle three, he strode in. 'Gordon Aspinall?'

'Yes.' The driver jerked to attention.

Poor coot. Rafe's keen gaze ran over the man's dejected body language. 'I'm Rafe Riccardi.' He offered his hand briefly and then turned aside to drag up another chair and sit opposite his patient. 'I'm covering for Dr Lyons while he's on leave,' he explained.

'I was hoping I could've seen Joe,' Gordon said awkwardly. 'We're both in the Rotary, like...'

'Sorry about that.' Reaching one hand back behind him, Rafe took Gordon's chart from the rack, perusing it swiftly.

'I understand you had a mishap with the school bus this morning?'

'Bit more than a mishap,' Gordon responded gruffly. 'Couple of the youngsters were injured.' His shoulders slumped. 'Mrs Holmes wants me charged.'

Rafe gave a bark of unamused laughter. 'Well, that's not for anyone but the police to decide. Have they been to talk to you yet?'

Gordon shook his head. 'Still at the accident scene, I reckon.'

'So, Gordon…' Rafe tossed the chart aside and leaned back in his chair '…how's your general health?'

'I feel OK most of the time. Not one to be taking sick days.'

'And what about this morning? Did you feel at any time you weren't in control of the bus? For instance, could you have blacked out for a second or two?'

Gordon pursed his lips thoughtfully. 'Might've got confused for a couple of seconds, I suppose.'

'In what way?'

'Hard to explain.'

'Take your time,' Rafe said gently. 'I'm not going anywhere.'

Gordon's pale blue eyes regarded the senior doctor steadily. 'There was a bit of wash-out on the side of the road. I tried to steer away from it but my hands wouldn't co-operate—felt kind of weak. So I went for the brakes but…my feet couldn't give me enough pressure. And then the bus just left the road and there was nothing I could do. It happened in a flash.'

'And there's no chance of mechanical failure?'

'The bus had a full service recently.' Gordon paused, clearly waiting for Rafe to start giving him some answers.

Instead, Rafe swung up from his chair, glancing up

as Toni came in quietly. He raised an eyebrow. 'Everything OK?'

She guessed he was asking whether Mrs Holmes had been placated. 'For the moment.' Toni wasn't about to let him off the hook just yet. She did think he'd been harsh with Kristal's mother. And arrogant.

Rafe lifted a shoulder indifferently. There were more important matters to be dealt with than whether he'd offended the Holmes woman. He turned his attention back to his patient. 'Gordon, I'm going to give you a general examination. I'll also be checking for any whiplash injury and any deficits in your hands and feet. Is that OK with you?'

'I suppose you gotta do what you gotta do.' Gordon sent a slightly trapped look at Toni.

'Just relax, Gordon.' Toni deliberately tried to infuse some lightness into the situation. 'We'll try to make it as easy as we can for you.'

Rafe reached for a stethoscope. 'Antonia, would you be good enough to record my findings, please?'

'Certainly, Doctor.' Toni took up the patient chart, unclipped her pen and waited.

Rafe's examination was painstaking, but he wasn't satisfied. 'OK, Gordon, you can hop down from the couch now.' His eyes narrowed as Gordon lowered his feet to the floor.

'And that's it, is it, Doc?' Gordon looked relieved.

'Not quite. I want you to walk for me, please. Just across to the far wall and back. Keep going until I ask you to stop.'

Gordon's eyes clouded. 'I haven't touched a drop of alcohol—'

'Just routine,' Rafe said easily. 'Will you walk now, please?' As Gordon walked, Rafe looked thoughtful, his mouth compressing as he watched. 'That's fine.' He held up his hand for Gordon to stop. 'Just one more thing and then we'll let you go. We'll need to take a blood sample from you.'

A few minutes later it was all done and Gordon was winding down his sleeve. 'When will I know something, Doc?'

'I'll have a chat with your GP first.' Rafe scribbled a notation on the chart and then watched as Toni labelled the blood and placed it aside for testing.

'We may need you back as early as this afternoon for a CT scan.'

All three turned as Liz popped her head in. 'The sergeant's just arrived to have a word with Gordon. Shall I ask him to wait?'

'No need. We're done here for the moment,' Rafe said. 'Use my office.'

Moving with quiet efficiency, Toni began putting the treatment room back to rights. 'You suspect the onset of Parkinson's, don't you?'

Rafe stroked a finger across his chin. 'It's looking that way. Several things are pointing to Gordon's co-ordination beginning to deteriorate.'

'So, why the blood test?' Toni stuffed the used linen into a receptacle. 'That won't help you make a diagnosis for Parkinson's. And it was obvious Gordon hadn't been drinking.'

Dark humour flickered in Rafe eyes and pulled at the corner of his mouth. 'Ever heard of covering our butts?' With a precise movement he thrust the chart at her and turned towards the doorway.

'Ra—fe…' His name died on her lips. He'd already gone.

CHAPTER TEN

TONI registered his departure with something like disbe-lief. How could he just walk out as though they had noth-ing to discuss? That they had nothing more than colleague status between them?

The fact that he so easily could, left her fuming. But what a fool she'd been, letting her personal life overlap into her professional life. Her mouth tightened. She'd done it again.

Disgust with herself hardened her resolve. She'd just have to tough it out. She'd done it before, after all. Giving the cubicle a cursory glance to make sure it was restored to order, she went back to the station.

Liz looked up from her paperwork. 'What's happen-ing with Gordon?'

Toni forced her mind to focus. 'More investigation. The reg is getting some history from his GP.'

The reg? Liz twitched an eyebrow. So formal. What on earth was going on with those two? 'Delegate and let's get a cuppa,' she said abruptly.

Toni looked dubious. 'I suppose we could...'

'You're the boss, Toni. Of course we could,' Liz sighed dramatically. 'I'm giving us permission.'

They took their tea and helped themselves to a couple of home-made muffins from a batch someone had brought in then made their way outside to the garden. 'This is more like it,' Liz said with satisfaction as they parked themselves at the outdoor table under a huge old elm. 'And we're only two minutes away if we're needed. We should do this more often, don't you agree?

Toni took a mouthful of her tea. 'You're about as transparent as a pane of glass, Lizzie. But you're right. I needed to get out of that place, if only briefly.'

For once Liz followed her instincts and kept silent, focusing on the garden sprinkler dancing silver in the sun.

After a while, Toni asked, 'Really and truly, Liz, why do we bother with men?'

'Because for most of the time we need them,' Liz responded mildly. 'And although they would rather take rat poison than admit it, *they* need us.'

More silence.

'Is everything OK with you and Rafe?' Liz asked.

Toni spanned her hands around her tea mug and looked into its depths. 'We've hit a bit of a rough patch.' More like a yawning chasm, she rephrased silently.

'You know if you want to talk…?' Liz offered.

Toni made a strangled sound in her throat. 'I wouldn't know where to start, Lizzie. But thanks…'

Damn Rafe Riccardi! Liz bit savagely into her muffin. If he'd hurt Toni, she, Elizabeth Carey, would personally have his guts for hair ribbons! 'You're owed plenty of leave,' she said. 'Why don't you just go home? Take the rest of the day off?'

'No, that's not me,' Toni refuted quietly. 'It's like running away. And I'm not doing that. Oh, Lizzie…' she shook her head '…I just want to thump some sense into him.'

Liz snorted inelegantly. 'I'd like a dollar for the number of times I've wanted to do exactly that to Matt.'

'You don't fight much, do you?' Toni's eyes widened in surprise.

Liz shrugged. 'Not now. But we did in our early days. Once I even packed a bag, took the kids and went home to Mum.'

'Oh, my stars! How long were you away?'

'About an hour. Matt came storming over with flowers. And not from the supermarket either.' She grinned reminiscently. 'The make-up sex was wild.'

Despite her problems, Toni laughed. 'Lizzie, you're priceless.'

'And so are you, my friend.' Suddenly serious, Liz leaned over and tapped Toni on the forearm. 'Don't ever forget that. Now, here's what we're going to do,' she said purposefully. 'If you won't go home, then let me deputise for the rest of the shift. Go and busy yourself elsewhere in the hospital. Have a wander through Kids. I believe young Harry is still in. Read him a story. Have a giggle. I'll deal with His Nibs if he asks.'

Toni felt her insides pinch. 'You won't say anything?

'Would I?' Liz sent her a wounded look. 'I can be the soul of discretion when it's needed.'

'I know,' Toni said, cheering up. 'That's why you're my trusted deputy.'

For the umpteenth time Rafe roamed through the department and back to his office. Antonia was keeping clear, that much was obvious. He balled his hands into fists of frustration. He couldn't believe how badly he was handling things with her. He knew she only wanted to help and it was purely his own stiff-necked pride that was keeping him from letting her. Perhaps it was the fact he didn't do trust very well—or not since Gabby...

But then why couldn't he get it into his head that Antonia was the antithesis of her, as Toni herself had already pointed out? With nothing resolved, he finished his shift and went home.

But when he went to bed, he could still smell her on his pillow—something so subtle it was barely there, but he couldn't breathe in enough of it. Face it. He growled a huff of self-derision. This is the closest you're going to get to her, mate, if you don't start taking control of your life.

Life had to go on, Toni resolved as she took handover next morning. She had to believe she and Rafe had a future. Somehow.

Casualty was busy, for which Toni was grateful. But with Justin and Grace well able to deal with any medical emergencies, Toni had no need to call Rafe. Nevertheless, she couldn't avoid him as he did his usual rounds but she exchanged only a brief good morning, almost *feeling* the weight of his gaze on her back as she hurried away.

If he'd looked taken aback, tough. She was all out of olive branches.

At the station Toni went through the charts from the morning. There'd been several walking wounded whose notes had to be sent on to their GPs...

'Toni, could I have a private word, please?'

Toni's gaze came up to see Harmony hovering nervously. 'Of course.' She got to her feet. 'My office?'

The young nurse nodded and followed as Toni led the way.

'Let's sit over here.' Toni indicated the informal cane setting near the window. When they were seated, she smiled. 'How can I help?'

Harmony rested her folded hands on the lacquered table top. 'I want to give in my notice.'

'You're leaving us?' Toni's brows twitched in query. 'Are you not happy here, Harmony?'

Harmony sent her boss a very straight look. 'I'm not enjoying being a nurse, Toni. It's not the staff here,' she was quick to add. 'You've all been lovely to me. It's just...' She stopped and bit her lip. 'I can't do it any more. I hate the smells and the noises the machines make.' She swallowed and grimaced. 'And the blood...'

Toni nodded. 'I understand. But there are other forms of nursing not necessarily in a hospital setting. Have you thought about that?'

'Not really. I mean, I like the patients—or most of them—and I like looking after people, but the clinical side of nursing is not for me.'

'That has to be your decision,' Toni said calmly. It was obvious Harmony had made up her mind. 'Have you any idea about what you'd really like to do?'

'I'm joining one of the airlines as cabin crew.' Harmony's cute dimple showed as she smiled. 'At least I will be as soon as I've undergone a medical and I need a couple of referees.' She paused. 'I wondered whether you would be one—if that's all right?' she tacked on quickly.

'No problem.' Toni flapped a hand. 'I'd be glad to, Harmony. But we'll be sorry to see you go. You really had the makings of a fine nurse. But I understand that it's not for everyone. Your patient skills were excellent and that will stand you in good stead as a flight attendant.'

'That's what attracted me to the job,' Harmony said seriously. 'And the interviewing panel commented on my people skills so I feel I'm making the right choice for me.'

Toni gave a wry smile. 'I dare say the corporate uniform is a lot smarter too. When do you want to finish?'

Harmony looked uncertain. 'I know it's mandatory to give two weeks' notice—'

'I'm sure we could waive that, if you need to get on with your own plans. You'll be based in Sydney, I take it?'

'Yes and I'm so looking forward to getting back.'

Toni left her chair and picked up the calendar from her deck. 'What say we make your finishing date a week from today?'

Harmony nodded enthusiastically. 'Thanks so much, Toni. Uh—about the references—do you think I could ask Dr Riccardi for one as well?'

Toni's gaze became shuttered. Just the mention of his name made every nerve in her body pinch and knot. 'I—' She stopped short when a cursory knock sounded on her door and Rafe himself poked his head in.

'Oh, sorry. I didn't mean to interrupt.'

'You're not.' Toni sent him a cool look. 'Harmony is leaving us. She was just wondering whether you would provide a character reference for her.'

'Of course.' Rafe's green gaze went from one to the other before he came in and parked himself against the window frame and crossed his feet at the ankles. 'Don't feel you're cut out for nursing, then, Harmony?' he asked lightly.

She dimpled up at the registrar. 'No. I'm joining an airline as cabin crew.'

Rafe gave a slight shrug. 'Good for you. Better than trying to struggle on in a situation when you're not happy.'

Toni felt her nerve ends, already raw, grate further. Was there a subtle message for her somewhere in there?

There was a beat of silence before Rafe continued, 'I guess you'll just need my phone number for the HR people, then, Harmony? That's the way it works nowadays, isn't it?'

'Thank you, yes.' Harmony blushed slightly. 'I can tell the others that I'm leaving, then?' She looked at Toni for confirmation.

'Feel free.' Toni dredged up a warm smile. 'And we

must have a farewell party for you. I'll ask Ed to organise something.'

'That'd be cool.' Harmony sounded youthfully eager.
'You'll come along won't you, Dr Riccardi?'

'Wouldn't miss it, Harmony.' Rafe extended his hand.
'Good luck. I hope everything goes well for you.'

With Harmony gone, so was their buffer and Rafe and
Toni stood facing one another.

'Was there something you wanted?' Toni finally asked.

Of course there was something he damned well wanted.
Rafe's mouth curled. 'You're determined to make this difficult, aren't you?'

Toni took a breath, stung by his accusation. She wanted
to yell at him but instead she went for a nonchalant shrug.
'You're doing a fine job of that yourself.'

'OK...' Rafe sighed and rubbed a hand through his hair.
If he didn't get this sorted, he'd go crazy. 'Could we talk?'

A swirl of emotions had Toni gripping the back of the
cane chair. *Talk.* Such a tiny word. The result of which
could either mean a new beginning for their relationship.
Or letting it go for ever. 'That's probably an excellent idea.'

Rafe held himself very still. 'Where and when, then?
You choose.'

'My place,' Toni said coolly. 'There's just one proviso,
Rafe.'

'What?' His head tilted at an angle that was almost arrogant until his eyes began taking in her bravely held little
chin, the soft curve of her cheek, the sweet, very sweet
fullness of her mouth. 'What...?' His voice descended into
soft appeal.

'That we actually talk.' Her mouth trembled infinitesimally. 'That means it's a two-way conversation with an
outcome. Is that clear?'

'Exceptionally.' Something like respect showed in Rafe's face. 'What time?'

'Eight o'clock.' Toni would have asked him for a meal but she knew neither of them would be able to eat it.

Rafe walked to the door and turned. 'I'll be there.'

As eight o'clock approached, Toni felt a lurching sensation in the pit of her stomach. And when the doorbell rang just after eight, she nearly jumped out of her skin.

She opened the door and let Rafe in. 'Thanks for coming,' she said quietly.

His brow rose briefly. He wasn't aware he'd had a choice. But he tamped down any desire to start the evening argumentatively.

'Would you mind coming through to the kitchen?' Toni asked. 'I'm making a cake for the hospital's street stall on Friday. I'd like to keep an eye on it.'

'Fine with me.' In the kitchen, he edgily accepted her offer of a glass of wine. 'Cake smells good.'

Very aware of him so close to her, Toni steadied her hand and carefully poured the wine. 'It's a chocolate mud cake,' she said. 'Well, it's a packet one but they're pretty good these days so no one will guess.' Handing him his glass of wine, she thought here they went again with another of those ridiculous conversations they were so good at.

They sat facing one another across the kitchen table, a heavy silence descending on them with the intensity of a fog rolling in from the ocean in winter.

'I don't want to start drawing up battle lines, Antonia.' Rafe stroked the stem of his glass with his thumb, his dark head bent over the golden liquid. 'I'd hope we could just...talk.'

Toni dragged in a deep breath. 'That's all I've ever

wanted to do.' When it seemed as though nothing more was forthcoming from him, she said with a flash of spirit, 'If you want out of this relationship, Rafe, then tell me. Let's end it cleanly.'

End it? Rafe felt a cramp in his chest. Is that what *she* wanted? The words went round and round in his head, thumping intolerably like a physical pain. 'For God's sake!' he rasped. 'I don't want to end it!'

'Oh. I thought...' Drawing back sharply, Toni looked into his anguished face.

'There's stuff I should have told you about.' Lifting a hand, he scrubbed the tips of fingers across his forehead. 'Stuff you had a right to know.'

Toni took a careful mouthful of her wine. 'Why did you feel you had to hide the fact you were have nightmares from me?'

'I didn't want to alarm you.'

'And we both know there's not a shred of credibility in that statement,' she threw at him. 'I've worked in Emergency for years. I hardly think a nightmare is going to alarm me.'

'OK.' He flicked a hand impatiently. 'Put it down to male ego or self-preservation. Or both.'

Toni softened. 'Has it been diagnosed as PTSD?'

He nodded.

'And what have they told you?'

'That the nightmares will probably stop of their own accord.'

Toni frowned. 'That's a bit open-ended, isn't it? Have you spoken to anyone since you've been back?'

He lifted a shoulder. 'I had a few sessions with a shrink. It helped. And I hadn't had a nightmare for weeks.'

'Well, that's positive, isn't it?' She sent him a guarded smile. And now he was out of the environment that had caused his stress in the first place, surely the chances of the nightmares recurring would diminish accordingly. 'Have you been given some strategies to enhance your well-being?'

He looked up, his jaw working. 'Swimming has been a great help.'

Well, of course it would be, Toni thought. Exercise in general was a proven method to enhance endorphins and reduce stress. She hesitated and then asked, 'Do you think the emergency with Harry brought stuff back into your subconscious?'

'It's possible. But I can't avoid treating children, Antonia.' His look was almost hostile.

'I'm not suggesting you do.' Toni willed herself to stay detached. 'Has my knowing made you feel uncomfortable?'

'It doesn't make me feel great.'

'Why is that? Do you think it makes you less of a person, less of a *man*, because you've experienced post-traumatic stress?'

He finished his wine in a couple of gulps. She was probably right but there was no way he wanted to go there.

'Couldn't it prove the opposite?' In an impatient gesture she shook her cascading hair back over her shoulders. 'That you're a compassionate human being, a dedicated doctor? Rafe, you have to know that any…condition that's not visible is isolating for the person concerned. It doesn't make you *odd,* for heaven's sake!'

He grunted a non-reply.

'I think you've done brilliantly.'

He sighed, managing a small smile. 'Really?'

'Yes.' She held out her hand and he took it, lacing their fingers. 'And you need to be realistic. This is a glitch. It's not as though you've lost an arm and your ability to practise medicine.'

He smiled crookedly. 'I like your logic, Antonia.'

'So, just keep tossing your baggage to me and we'll handle it together. Deal?'

Rafe felt the crippling weight of indecision fall away. He should have been upfront with her weeks ago. Trusted her. He'd do better from now on. Hell, he'd better. He didn't think she'd offer him too many more chances. 'Deal,' he said.

The days were rushing by with a speed that was leaving Toni almost breathless. Harmony was long gone and had been replaced by a nice young RN, David Kerwin, who was three years post-grad and who seemed to be fitting into their team very well.

And Rafe's term was drawing to a close. Only a few weeks to go now. And with every day that passed, Toni's good sense was struggling to retain ascendancy over her impatience about the future. She wasn't aware Rafe had made any plans. Well, if he had, he hadn't told her. And she'd thought they'd got over all those hurdles of not communicating.

She wanted a future with him but she wasn't about to push. Perhaps she could gently instigate a discussion about it, she thought. Maybe tonight. She looked at her watch and gave a half-smile. Why wait until night? They were both due a break. They could grab a few bits and pieces from the canteen and go across to the park. Relaxed under one of the beautiful old gum trees, the mellow hint of autumn in the air, who knew? Rafe might just start talking about the future…their future.

Together.

Leaving her office, she went back to the station. 'I'm taking the early lunch, Lizzie.'

Liz looked up from the computer. 'Go for it,' she said absently. 'Oh, we should probably have a think about a send-off for Rafe. Time's running out. Have you two made any plans?'

'Not yet.' Toni tried to look unconcerned. 'Still up in the air a bit. It'll sort itself out.'

'Of course it will.' She sent Toni a provocative, Liz-like grin. 'Wouldn't hurt to give him a nudge, you know.'

Toni flicked a smile in return. 'You read my mind.' Holding the thought, she went along to Rafe's office, tapped and poked her head in. He looked up from his computer and beckoned her in.

'Just finishing an email,' he said. 'Won't be a second.'

Toni went to stand behind him, her hands automatically smoothing across the breadth of his shoulders. Bending, she smudged a kiss on his nape, only to feel him make a restive movement before he hit 'Send' and then swung round on his chair to face her. 'I was just coming to find you. We need to talk.'

'Snap.' Tony smiled. 'I was on the same wavelength. I thought we could have lunch in the park.'

'Uh—can't, sorry.' Abruptly, he swung off his chair and went to stand against the window, facing her, his hands pressed down on the sill. 'A lot has happened over the last twelve hours, Antonia.'

Toni felt an immediate lick of unease. His demeanour showed...*excitement.* And somehow it didn't seem the kind she could share. She swallowed unevenly. 'Better tell me, then.'

'Last night I had a call from Ari Cohen, my former boss in Siem Reap. They have an outbreak of whooping cough among the children. The need to do a mass inoculation is critically urgent. He's asked me to go over and help.'

Toni felt all the strength drain from her legs. So this was yet another hurdle they had to negotiate. Would it ever end? She drew in all her powers of self-protection. 'Surely they have trained people to do that. Why you?'

'Because I'm already accredited to work there. They have recruits coming on line but they have to be brought up to speed. And this is an emergency.'

'And you're going.'

'Yes.' A muscle pulled in his jaw. 'If the inoculation programme isn't carried out, it'll be a catastrophe.'

But why did he think it was down to him to take all the responsibility? Why? Toni fought for calm. 'Won't you need medical clearance?'

'Keith took care of that this morning.'

'Did you tell him about the nightmares?'

'They've stopped.'

Well, she only had his word for that. It wasn't as though they spent every night together. 'Aren't you risking your complete recovery by going back into that environment? Don't they care?'

His dark brows shot together. 'Of course they care! In fact, Ari stressed the point.' Rafe hesitated as if searching for the right words. 'Antonia, this is something I need to do.'

'And what about us?' Toni demanded, her eyes flashing. To hell with him and what he *needed* to do. 'Did you even think to talk about this with me before you just decided to go?'

'I'm talking to you now!' Rafe's voice rose. 'Antonia, this couldn't wait. Surely, as a health professional, you can understand that?'

Well, she could and she couldn't. 'You know I play

straight, Rafe. You know that! If the situation had been reversed, I would have come to you first, before I decided anything. So what do I actually mean to you? It seems to me I've been nothing more than a convenient bedmate!'

Rafe recoiled as if she'd slapped him. 'That remark is not worthy of you, Toni. Not worthy of us, of what we've shared. I care deeply about you. You have to know that. And I *will* be back.'

'The hell you will.' Her voice hardened. 'Once you get back there, it will consume you again.' Toni's throat felt like sandpaper as she swallowed. But she hadn't finished. 'What about your commitments to the hospital here? Are you walking out on them as well?'

'They're covered.' His mouth snapped shut, his tightly clamped lips a harsh line across his face. 'And Joe will be back in a couple of weeks.'

She looked at him, her eyes unguarded. 'When do you go?'

'I'm driving to Sydney this afternoon, flying out tomorrow morning. You've—uh—left some of your things at the annexe...' His throat jerked as he swallowed. 'I'll leave the key in the usual place so you can collect them whenever...'

'When you've gone.'

'Antonia, please believe me, none of this is meant to hurt you.' He moved to hold her but she waved him away, although she hoped he wouldn't guess what it cost her to pull away from the reassurance of those warm, strong arms.

'It's too late, Rafe.'

'It needn't be.'

Oh, but it was and they both knew it. 'Just...stay well...' Blindly, she began making her way across to the door.

'Toni!' Rafe leapt after her as though he could actually halt her desperation. 'Don't leave like this.'

Hand on the doorknob, she turned. She gave a sad little shake of her head. 'I'm not the one leaving, Rafe. *You* are.'

Safely outside his office, Toni almost ran back to the nurses' station, the drum-heavy thud in her heart almost suffocating her. In just a few minutes Rafe had turned her life on its head. And he'd had the hide to say he cared!

'Oh, lord!' Liz jumped up from her chair. 'Toni, what's wrong?'

Toni threw caution to the winds. It would be all over the hospital shortly. 'He's leaving, Lizzie. Going back to Cambodia.'

Liz swore quietly and pithily. 'You look in shock.' Liz quickly guided Toni into an empty cubicle. 'Sit down,' she ordered, pulling the screen for privacy. 'I'll get you a glass of water.'

'Now, tell me what happened,' Liz coaxed a little while later. 'If you want to,' she added diplomatically.

Toni filled her friend in as best she could. 'He says he'll be back,' she ended with a mirthless little huff.

'And you don't believe him?'

'Would you?' Toni shook her head. 'Once he's there it's obvious it will take over his life again.'

Liz bit her lip. So Matt's prediction had been right. But she couldn't stick another knife into Toni and remind her of that. 'You could be wrong, you know,' she said instead.

'Yeah…' Toni felt her heart shrink even further. 'If you believe in fairy-tales.'

'Go home, Toni.' Liz's tone brooked no argument. 'You don't need to be here.'

Toni nodded listlessly. 'I think I will.'

Rafe fell back into his chair as if his strings had been cut. God, what a disaster. He hadn't expected Toni's reaction. He'd wanted her onside about his decision. Surely she should have been able to understand he needed to do this. Apart from the medical emergency, he had to, if ever he was to be truly whole again. He pressed his fingers across his eyes as if staving off pain. 'How could she think I didn't love her?' he rasped under his breath. Hell, I'm doing this for her as well as myself. I'm doing it for *us*.

When his phone rang, he reached out groggily and picked it up. 'Yes, Maureen.'

'I've confirmed your flight to Bangkok, Rafe.'

'Could I have the flight number please?' He scribbled down the information. 'And the connecting flight to Seim Reap?'

'I was able to do that as well.'

'Good. What's the arrival time for that? Thanks, got all that. I'll email MSF and pass on the details.'

'Safe trip, then…'

'Maureen, thanks for everything.' Rafe took a steadying breath. 'You've been great.' Replacing the receiver, he got slowly to his feet.

Now he had to tell the team.

CHAPTER ELEVEN

In her office, Toni finished writing up the shift rosters for another month. Logging off the computer, she looked into space.

It seemed half a lifetime since Rafe had left but in reality it was only a matter of weeks. And despite her best efforts to block him out, to restart her life, her thoughts, especially at night, would push past the block she'd striven to make Rafe-proof. The heady feeling of completeness she'd felt with him would ambush her out of nowhere.

Maybe he'd loved her in his way, she thought now. But he walked to a different drummer. And she couldn't walk with him. *But why couldn't she? Why?* The sudden thought almost her made her dizzy. A reed of hope as slender as a gossamer strand sprang in her heart as the thought took hold.

She'd been so self-involved, she owned with something like shame. So…insular. Rafe had wanted to do something good, something worthwhile with his medical skills. Why couldn't she have understood that? She thought back to the day when he'd tried to explain his reasons for going. But instead of listening, she'd taken the high moral ground.

And walked out on him.

She closed her eyes. She wanted to turn back the clock.

Spin the hands into reverse. But she couldn't do that. But there was something she could do—she could go to him…

'OK…' She exhaled a deep breath. First things first.

Aware of the accelerated beat of her heart, she picked up the phone to call the DON.

'Loretta, I need to take some leave. Well, whatever's owing to me and as soon as you can arrange it, please. A family matter I have to deal with,' Toni said, forgiving herself the white lie. 'No, I'll hold.' Her fingers tightened on the phone as she waited. 'Today?' Toni felt her heart go into freefall. 'Thank you so much, Loretta. Thank you…'

Toni had barely put the phone down when Liz burst in. Without ceremony, she spun out a chair and sat facing Toni across the desk. 'I've just got off the phone with Loretta,' she said. 'Apparently I'm to be acting NUM for the next three weeks. Care to tell me what's going on?'

'I think you can guess, Lizzie. I'm going to Rafe.'

Liz blinked her uncertainty. 'Have you heard from him?'

Toni shook her head.

'So, you're just going over there…' Liz made a vague rocking movement with her hand. 'Shouldn't you try to call him first?'

'I need to see him.'

Liz sucked down on her bottom lip in consternation. 'I worry for you, Toni. Have you thought about what you're doing?'

'No, Lizzie, I haven't. It was a snap decision. But I'm slowly going nuts just hanging about in limbo. I love him. I have to find out of he loves me.'

'OK…' Liz expelled a deep breath. 'I can see you've made up your mind.' She looked at her watch. 'The shift's only got an hour to run. Why don't you take off? Whizz up town and see the travel agent and get your flights booked.'

'Would you mind?' Toni was already getting to her feet.

'Of course I don't mind,' Liz said, whirling upright as well. 'Anyway, I'm the boss as of ten minutes ago. So, Ms Morell, you have my permission to take an early mark. And if you need help of any kind, call me,' Liz insisted. 'Matt has contacts all over the place.'

The two friends hugged briefly. 'Thanks, Lizzie...' Toni clamped her lips to stop them trembling. It was really happening. She was going to Rafe.

She only hoped he'd still want her. As much as she wanted him.

Toni had read her travel guide from cover to cover on her flight from Sydney to Bangkok. And on the connecting flight to Seim Reap, her excitement grew until it was almost combustible. But there was trepidation as well. Perhaps she should have let Rafe know of her impending arrival...

Because she'd wanted somewhere lovely for her and Rafe to be together, she'd booked at one of Seim Reap's upmarket hotels, surprised and delighted with her suite. Now, she just had to let him know she was here.

She couldn't waste any more time in conjecture. Hoping he still had his cellphone and that it worked here, she dialled his number and waited, prepared for it to go to voicemail, but it was picked up almost immediately.

'Dr Riccardi.'

'Rafe...? It's me...' She swallowed the huskiness of nerves.

'Antonia?' His voice was laced with amazement. 'Where are you?'

'I'm here in Seim Reap. Could we catch up—I mean, if you want to...?'

He was noncommittal. 'Where are you staying?'

She told him the name of the boutique hotel.

'I'll be right over.'

'But aren't you at the hospital?'

'I'm off duty.'

'Oh.' Her composure slipped every which way. In a matter of minutes she could be in his arms. Or not. He hadn't sounded exactly thrilled. 'I'm in an outdoor lounge near the pool—'

'Fine. Don't move.'

As if she could. Toni felt her legs turn to jelly as she turned from the railing and took a chair at one of the tables, facing the entrance that was delineated by an archway of tropical ferns and twining deep purple bougainvilleas.

And steeled herself for the most important meeting of her life.

Rafe's heart was clamouring as he took to the street, making his way through the endless bustle to Antonia's hotel. After the way they'd parted, he couldn't believe she was here. Surely she'd come to reconcile. Surely. Why else? But old habits died hard so he'd make no assumptions. Play it cool. But his heart was far from playing it cool. Instead it thumped against his chest wall like a native drum as he crossed the bridge over the lotus pond and entered the hotel's walled garden.

Toni's breathing almost hitched to a halt when she saw him weaving his way through the pre-lunch crowd that was beginning to gather. He was wearing chinos and a pale blue cotton shirt. And looked so familiar her heart ached just at seeing him. She stood to greet him, wanting to throw herself into his arms. But her guide book on protocol had decreed that overt displays of affection were considered disrespectful. Instead, she waited.

Seeing her standing there, in her long cotton skirt and

simple button-down blouse, Rafe took a breath so deep it hurt, causing his heart to knock harder against his ribs. He wanted to vault over the tables and run to her, gather her up. But that kind of behaviour would be frowned on here. Instead, he held himself in check. After all, she mightn't want to be *gathered* up, he reminded himself in a swift reality check. After the way they'd parted, nothing was certain here. Nothing.

'Hi...' Toni felt heat high on cheekbones as he stood in front of her.

Rafe moved a hand to brush her cheek but pulled it back before it could connect. Instead, he took both her hands and held them loosely. He looked down at her.

'I'm real,' she said on a jagged laugh.

'I know...' His eyes burned like emeralds. 'When did you arrive?'

'Couple of hours ago. The hotel's a bit posh,' she said, as if she needed to explain. 'But the travel agent said it was safe because I was on my own...'

'It's a good place. Our World Health people always stay here when they visit.'

She nodded. And this was yet another of these ridiculous conversations they seemed destined to have. 'Shall we sit down?'

'Ah...' He looked around, letting her hands go and planting them on his hips. 'It's nearly lunchtime. Would you like a drink?'

'That'd be nice.'

'Lager? It goes well with Asian food.'

She managed a fleeting smile. 'Fine.'

Rafe returned with the glasses of icy cold beer.

Toni picked up her glass. 'What should we drink to?'

Determined to keep things low-key until he knew where

he stood—where they stood—he said, 'Let's drink to a happy holiday for you. How long are you staying?'

'Five days. It was a package offer.' And I wasn't sure how long I'd need to set things right between us, Toni added silently.

'You can see a lot in five days,' Rafe said helpfully. 'Angkor Wat is a must see for any tourist. I'm sure the hotel will arrange a guide for you.'

She'd read about the amazing temple complex in her guide book and had been hoping Rafe would visit it with her. But, of course, if he was working... 'You've been there?'

'Many times. It's heart-stopping. The guide will explain the significance of every Hindu and Buddhist god. Both religions receive tribute there. And you won't have seen anything like the giant kapok trees. And the markets are fantastic.'

Toni felt her eyes glaze. This was going right over her head. Rafe was sounding like a tourist guide himself. She hated it but she was at a loss to know what to say to feel close with him again. 'You look well,' she managed at last.

'I *am* well.' He hitched a shoulder impatiently. Hell, had she come to check up on his health? Was that it? Suddenly the atmosphere between them was crackling with instability.

'And the inoculation programme?' Toni ploughed on.

He blinked. 'Sorry?'

'The inoculation programme.'

He gave a tight shrug. 'We've managed to contain the spread of the disease. Unfortunately, we lost a few of the children but that was inevitable.'

And he seemed calm about it. Philosophical. Professional. Toni felt lost in a sea of confusion. He had his life back on track. He belonged here. And she felt alienated, foolish. For once her instincts had let her down. She had to make her escape. Be anywhere but here. With him. 'I shouldn't have come here…' she whispered through a throat so tight it hurt.

Rafe took such a deep breath his chest heaved. The pain in her words grabbed at his gut. He still felt stunned seeing her after all this time. And thrown right out of his comfort zone. 'Then why exactly did you come, Antonia?'

She gave a bitter laugh. 'Well, silly me, I missed you. And I thought there might still be a chance for us. But I see I was wrong. You're obviously in your element here. You've moved on.' She half rose. 'And I think it's time I do as well.'

'Toni, wait! Don't go making assumptions. I'm a bit stunned that you've come all this way…' Stunned? He was poleaxed. 'Don't go. Please…' His voice was rough, halfway between a whisper and a groan. He looked around wildly. 'We need to go somewhere and talk.'

'I have a room…' Her voice shook.

'Give me the number and go up. I'll book on the same floor.' His gaze shimmered over her. 'And then I'll come to you. It'll be better that way.'

Protocol again. Toni bit her lip. 'You don't have any luggage.'

'It won't be a problem. They know me here. I'll tell them my luggage is on its way. And it would be. He knew that for certain.

Toni felt a wild mix of emotions tumble around inside her as she waited for Rafe. She walked out onto her balcony, turned round and walked back inside. Oh, lord, it was like waiting for a first date to arrive.

When the soft knock came on her door, she took a deep

breath and went to let him in. 'Hello.' Her voice was a breath of sound. 'Have you checked in?'

'Yes.' He reached out, moving his hands very gently beneath the silky fall of her hair, encircling her nape.

Toni felt herself trembling, vibrations moving through her body as his mouth trailed down from her temple, across her cheek, finally taking and closing in on her mouth.

With an urgent need throbbing down low in her body she sank into his arms and they were kissing like they'd never kissed before.

'Oh, Rafe…' Toni finally eased away, blinking the sudden tears from her eyes. 'I'm so sorry about the way we parted. I walked out on you.'

'You don't need to apologise,' he said softly. 'I'm not without fault. I went at everything like a bull at a gate.'

'But I was so…judgmental. I should have understood you had important work to do here.'

'And I should have been more upfront from the beginning.' He heaved in a long breath and let it go. 'I love you, Antonia. And that's what I should have spelled out before I left.'

Toni's heart beat faster at the sincerity of his declaration and the words she'd so longed to hear. 'And I would have told you right back.'

His green eyes glinted. 'So, say it now.'

'I…love you, Rafe. Oh, I do.' It felt such a relief to be able to say it that she laughed.

He smiled down into her happy face. 'We're sorted, then?'

'I think we are, aren't we?'

The curve of her bottom felt good snuggled into his palms and he nodded. 'So, how are we going to spend these five days of your holiday?'

'Well…' She fiddled with the button on his shirt front.

'Perhaps I could just fit in around your duty hours at the hospital. You're not working every minute, are you?'

'I'm not working at all,' he said. 'I finished yesterday. My work here is done. I was coming home. To you.'

'Oh...' She snuggled closer. 'Then we were both on the same mission.'

'It seems like it,' he said softly, touching a hand to her hair, lingering over its softness. 'And just so we have things straight, and I don't care what it takes, I'm never letting you go again.'

Joy, clear and pure, streamed through her. 'And that goes for me as well. I'm not letting *you* go, either, Rafe Riccardi.' She frowned a bit. 'I can't believe the needless unhappiness we've put each other through—'

'Hush,' he said, placing his finger on her lips. 'No looking back. This is our whole new beginning.'

'Then where better to start it than here in this beautiful place? Come and look,' she invited, gently disengaging from his arms and holding out her hand. 'This is what's called a spa suite,' she said almost shyly. 'The bath is almost big as a car.'

'Never mind the bath.' Desire was roaring through him like a storm. He had his brave, beautiful Antonia back. He wanted just to hold her, love her as she deserved to be loved. He tipped up her chin before urgently caressing her mouth. 'Does this place have a bed?'

'What a silly question.' Very slowly, she began to unbutton his shirt, all the while staring up into his tautened face. With his shirt hanging open, she began moving her hands in caressing little semi-circles over the tanned skin of his chest. 'Shall we try it out?'

His gaze deepened and darkened. 'I think it would be very remiss of us not to.'

* * *

Next morning.

Rafe and Toni were enjoying breakfast on the poolside deck at the hotel. 'This fruit is truly fabulous,' she said, as the red papaya melted against her tongue.

'And so was last night.' His look was tender. 'You continue to amaze me, Antonia.'

She wrinkled her nose at him but her smile was tender in return. 'What are we doing today?'

He dug into his blueberry pancake with obvious pleasure. 'Any preference?'

'I want to get some presents to take home.'

'So, the markets? What else?'

She hesitated, not sure how he would react to her request. 'I'd like to see your hospital.'

He brought his head up slowly. It was the last thing he'd thought she'd want to do. 'Are you sure? I mean, you're on holidays.'

She flicked a hand in dismissal. 'I need to see for myself the kind of work you've done here, Rafe. It's all part of who you are. It would mean a lot to me.'

'No problem. We can do that. You can meet Ari. I've told him all about you.'

Toni looked taken aback. 'What did you tell him?'

Rafe hitched a shoulder in a shrug. 'Just that you were the most beautiful woman in the world and that I'd stuffed things up with you. And that as soon as my work was done, I was going home to Australia to win you back.'

'Oh, my God…' She took his outstretched hand across the table. 'I don't know what to say.'

'What do you think about marriage?' He expelled the words as though they might have burned him.

Toni blinked. *Wow*, this was right out of left field. 'In general or to you?'

His grip on her hand tightened. 'Don't split hairs, Ms Morell. To me, of course.'

She smiled mistily. 'I think it would be lovely. But what about you? Is it something you want to do again?'

'With my history, you mean?'

'It has to be the right decision for you,' Toni insisted.

'OK…' Rafe knew there were still words to be said, answers to be given. Hearts to be bared and made whole again. 'What I had with Gabrielle was nothing like a marriage should have been. I know that now. But with you…' He stopped and looked at her. 'So different.' He shook his head as if it still amazed him. 'You light up my life.'

'I think that's a song.'

He smiled. 'And there I was thinking I was getting better at expressing my feelings.'

'I think you do wonderfully well.' She looked into his eyes, seeing the sheen of tenderness. 'You make me feel so loved, Rafe.'

'I always will,' he promised. 'Uh—I have something for you.' He reached into his shirt pocket and pulled out a tiny silk bag. 'I was going to give you this when I got back home—that's if you still wanted—well, I'd like you to have it now…with my love.'

Heart overflowing, Toni took the scrap of silk and opened the drawstring at the top. 'It's a ring…'

'Well, fancy that,' he mocked, but gently. 'I had it made especially.'

'It's beautiful.' Toni looked down at the exquisitely fashioned ring. It was wide, with a lotus flower edged with tiny diamonds in the centre on a band of white gold studded with sapphires. 'Oh, Rafe…I love it…'

He gave an audible sigh of relief. 'That's one hurdle over.' He held out his hand for the ring and slipped it on her finger. His gaze held hers steadily. 'Will you marry me, Antonia?'

She nodded, too close to the edge to speak.

Grinning, Raph cupped a hand to his ear. 'Sorry, I didn't quite get that.'

Toni batted the happy tears away, her new ring sparkling as it caught the morning sun. 'Yes, I'll marry you, Rafe.' She managed a watery smile. 'I can't believe we're doing this over breakfast in a public place. I can't even kiss you.'

He took her hand as if reaffirming their commitment. 'We'll make up for it later. Where do you want to get married?'

Toni looked dreamily at her ring. 'I've always thought St Anne's would be pretty special. And it's where we first... connected, if you recall?'

He nodded. 'St Anne's it is then.'

'Have you booked your flight home?' Toni asked.

'Not yet. And now that you're here, we could fly home together.'

'And in the immediate future...' She paused. 'Where is *home* going to be for us?'

'Ah...' He took her hand again. 'I need to talk to you about that.'

Toni felt an odd glitch in her breathing. That sounded a bit ominous. What if he wanted to go on working in the developing world? Could she work by his side, live his dream with him? There was only one answer. Of course she could. They were matching parts of the same whole. He was her *one*. 'Better talk to me, then,' she said carefully.

'You realise Joe is back at Forrestdale?'

'Of course. They had a wonderful time in Italy.'

'But it seems the trip has left them with a taste for adventure. He and the family want to move on.'

'They do?' Toni was startled. 'He's not said anything—neither has Cath. How do you know all this?'

Rafe's mouth drew in. 'We've been in touch. Joe's been offered a senior post at the Randwick in Sydney. But the board at Forrestdale won't release him until they have a replacement.'

Toni looked wide-eyed as everything began falling into place. 'Are you thinking of applying, by any chance?'

'I am. But ultimately it has to be a joint decision for us.'

Toni could hardly believe the joy she felt. 'I think it would be amazing to begin our lives together in Forrestdale, amongst our friends.'

Rafe's green gaze lit. 'So, I'll go ahead and speak to Bernie?'

She nodded happily.

'I might not get it, of course,' he warned.

Toni made a not-too-polite huff of disbelief. 'Bernie will boast he headhunted you.'

Rafe chuckled. 'It feels good to be going back home together, doesn't it.'

'Magic.' She looked dreamy and then sobered. 'Is working at Forrestdale going to be enough for you, Rafe? I mean, career-wise'

'Are you asking if I want to keep working for MSF?'

'I suppose… But I want you to know that if you do, even occasionally, I'll go with you.'

'Thank you for that.' His eyes squeezed shut and when he opened them they were lit with purpose. 'I feel rewarded in countless ways that I've been able to use my medical training to help the less fortunate. And I'll never forget it. But that part of my life is over now. I need to put down roots. With you.'

Toni felt she was overdosing on sheer happiness. 'We'll have to get a home in Forrestdale, then.'

'Well—we kind of have one,' he said vaguely. 'Joe and Cath want to sell. I put in an offer. But I wouldn't have done anything definite without your approval,' he added hurriedly.

Toni's eyes opened wide in amazement. 'But I'd love to live in that beautiful home. We could have an amazing life there. Raise our family there.' Her gaze faltered. 'You'd like children, wouldn't you, Rafe?'

Looking at her, so sweet and sexy in her cheesecloth shirt open all the way down and the snug little vest top underneath showing just a peep of cleavage, Rafe knew a certainty he wouldn't have believed a year ago. He felt as though he had the world in his hands. He'd never felt so...grounded. Loving Antonia had changed his life. And with her as their mother, their children would be amazingly loved and bright and beautiful. 'I'd love us to have kids,' he said throatily. 'All this is meant to be, Antonia. I've never been so sure of anything in my life. I promise to be true to you and make you happy.'

'Then right back at you, Riccardi.' She smiled, her gaze as clear and soft as the air around them. Reaching for the delicate porcelain teapot, she began to pour. 'Now, I wouldn't want to rush my future husband, but don't you have a phone call to make?'

* * * * *

Mills & Boon® Hardback

October 2012

ROMANCE

Banished to the Harem	Carol Marinelli
Not Just the Greek's Wife	Lucy Monroe
A Delicious Deception	Elizabeth Power
Painted the Other Woman	Julia James
A Game of Vows	Maisey Yates
A Devil in Disguise	Caitlin Crews
Revelations of the Night Before	Lynn Raye Harris
Defying her Desert Duty	Annie West
The Wedding Must Go On	Robyn Grady
The Devil and the Deep	Amy Andrews
Taming the Brooding Cattleman	Marion Lennox
The Rancher's Unexpected Family	Myrna Mackenzie
Single Dad's Holiday Wedding	Patricia Thayer
Nanny for the Millionaire's Twins	Susan Meier
Truth-Or-Date.com	Nina Harrington
Wedding Date with Mr Wrong	Nicola Marsh
The Family Who Made Him Whole	Jennifer Taylor
The Doctor Meets Her Match	Annie Claydon

MEDICAL

A Socialite's Christmas Wish	Lucy Clark
Redeeming Dr Riccardi	Leah Martyn
The Doctor's Lost-and-Found Heart	Dianne Drake
The Man Who Wouldn't Marry	Tina Beckett

ROMANCE

A Secret Disgrace	Penny Jordan
The Dark Side of Desire	Julia James
The Forbidden Ferrara	Sarah Morgan
The Truth Behind his Touch	Cathy Williams
Plain Jane in the Spotlight	Lucy Gordon
Battle for the Soldier's Heart	Cara Colter
The Navy SEAL's Bride	Soraya Lane
My Greek Island Fling	Nina Harrington
Enemies at the Altar	Melanie Milburne
In the Italian's Sights	Helen Brooks
In Defiance of Duty	Caitlin Crews

HISTORICAL

The Duchess Hunt	Elizabeth Beacon
Marriage of Mercy	Carla Kelly
Unbuttoning Miss Hardwick	Deb Marlowe
Chained to the Barbarian	Carol Townend
My Fair Concubine	Jeannie Lin

MEDICAL

Georgie's Big Greek Wedding?	Emily Forbes
The Nurse's Not-So-Secret Scandal	Wendy S. Marcus
Dr Right All Along	Joanna Neil
Summer With A French Surgeon	Margaret Barker
Sydney Harbour Hospital: Tom's Redemption	Fiona Lowe
Doctor on Her Doorstep	Annie Claydon

Mills & Boon® Hardback

November 2012

ROMANCE

A Night of No Return	Sarah Morgan
A Tempestuous Temptation	Cathy Williams
Back in the Headlines	Sharon Kendrick
A Taste of the Untamed	Susan Stephens
Exquisite Revenge	Abby Green
Beneath the Veil of Paradise	Kate Hewitt
Surrendering All But Her Heart	Melanie Milburne
Innocent of His Claim	Janette Kenny
The Price of Fame	Anne Oliver
One Night, So Pregnant!	Heidi Rice
The Count's Christmas Baby	Rebecca Winters
His Larkville Cinderella	Melissa McClone
The Nanny Who Saved Christmas	Michelle Douglas
Snowed in at the Ranch	Cara Colter
Hitched!	Jessica Hart
Once A Rebel...	Nikki Logan
A Doctor, A Fling & A Wedding Ring	Fiona McArthur
Her Christmas Eve Diamond	Scarlet Wilson

MEDICAL

Maybe This Christmas...?	Alison Roberts
Dr Chandler's Sleeping Beauty	Melanie Milburne
Newborn Baby For Christmas	Fiona Lowe
The War Hero's Locked-Away Heart	Louisa George

Mills & Boon® Large Print

November 2012

ROMANCE

The Secrets She Carried	Lynne Graham
To Love, Honour and Betray	Jennie Lucas
Heart of a Desert Warrior	Lucy Monroe
Unnoticed and Untouched	Lynn Raye Harris
Argentinian in the Outback	Margaret Way
The Sheikh's Jewel	Melissa James
The Rebel Rancher	Donna Alward
Always the Best Man	Fiona Harper
A Royal World Apart	Maisey Yates
Distracted by her Virtue	Maggie Cox
The Count's Prize	Christina Hollis

HISTORICAL

An Escapade and an Engagement	Annie Burrows
The Laird's Forbidden Lady	Ann Lethbridge
His Makeshift Wife	Anne Ashley
The Captain and the Wallflower	Lyn Stone
Tempted by the Highland Warrior	Michelle Willingham

MEDICAL

Sydney Harbour Hospital: Lexi's Secret	Melanie Milburne
West Wing to Maternity Wing!	Scarlet Wilson
Diamond Ring for the Ice Queen	Lucy Clark
No.1 Dad in Texas	Dianne Drake
The Dangers of Dating Your Boss	Sue MacKay
The Doctor, His Daughter and Me	Leonie Knight